The Zodiac Cases
of
Sherlock Holmes

Volume 1

Aries, Taurus, Gemini, Cancer, Leo & Virgo

From the Notes of
John H. Watson M.D.

Edited by
Roger Riccard

First published in 2025 by
The Irregular Special Press
for Baker Street Studios Ltd
Endeavour House
170 Woodland Road, Sawston
Cambridge, CB22 3DX, UK

ISBN: 978 1 901091 97 7

Illustrations: Prismis 24-1, the brightest point of light at the centre of the NGC 6357 region,
and the zodiac map used for the cover both courtesy of Wikimedia Commons as are the icons
used internally.

Typeset in 8/11/20pt Palatino

About the Author

Roger Riccard has Scottish roots, which trace his lineage back to the Roses of Highland, Scotland. This ancestry encouraged his interest in the writings of Sir Arthur Conan Doyle. He has now surpassed Doyle's total of sixty stories featuring the world's first consulting detective.

He lives in a suburb of Los Angeles with two cats named Bela (after Bela Lugosi who played Dracula, because he likes to bite) and Amanda (after Amanda Blake who played Miss Kitty on the old television western series, *Gunsmoke*).

When not editing Watson's notes of Sherlock Holmes's adventures, he is singing in a musical group that entertains senior citizens in retirement homes. He also works with GriefShare as a facilitator for grieving families.

Information and news about his works can be found at www.sherlockriccard.com.

To My Rosilyn,
My One and Only Aquarian

Note to the Reader

As with all the stories I put forth about the world's first consulting detective, Mr. Sherlock Holmes, I must give thanks and credit to his original chronicler, Dr. John H. Watson. While not all his notes are complete, or in some cases, orderly, those which were left to Mrs. Hudson's care and subsequently entrusted to her grandniece, my 'Grandma Ruby (*nee* Hudson)' of New York, in the days leading up to World War II, have provided the essential facts of the tales herein. I have attempted to flesh out historical and geographical details via research and networking with other Sherlockians and British associates. I beg the reader's indulgence for any errors and trust that the stories shall be entertaining in and of themselves.

Roger Riccard
Los Angeles, CA USA

Contents

Aries: The Ram
(21st March – 19th April)

A Reckoning at Ramsgate

There is nothing that an Aries cannot achieve once they set their mind to it – no mountain is too high. However, as competitive as they are, they are also insecure. You may find them nursing a hidden imposter syndrome that can chip away at their confidence if allowed free rein.

Chapter One

It was October 1901. Autumn leaves were changing their colours and the weather in London was beginning to cool as my flatmate, the consulting detective, Sherlock Holmes and I sat before an evening fire at 221B Baker Street. The smell of roasting beef and freshly baked bread wafted up from our landlady's kitchen. Mrs. Hudson's footsteps could be heard on the stairs, and she soon opened the door to deliver the last post of the day.

"There's one here for you, Dr. Watson," she said. "The other two are for 'The Detective Sherlock Holmes'." She smiled as she put them into my hands, I being the closest to the door. "Dinner will be ready in half an hour."

I tossed the letters addressed to my friend into his lap as I returned to my seat, having stood at Mrs. Hudson's arrival. He frowned at me, glanced at them, set them on the table next to him and continued to smoke away at his briarwood pipe as he contemplated whatever problem was occupying his mind presently.

For myself, I was intrigued by the coat of arms on the back of the envelope addressed to 'Doctor John Watson'. It was a design that I had not seen in over twenty years but recognised immediately as I had witnessed the Westwood arms on nearly a daily basis while serving on the medical staff of the Fifth Northumberland Fusiliers in Afghanistan. Major Cornell Westwood was our commanding officer at the field hospital.

However, when I again looked at the front of the envelope, the handwriting was distinctly that of a woman. I opened the envelope and withdrew the letter, also written in the same feminine hand.

Dear Dr. Watson,

My name is Victoria Westwood and I am the daughter of your former commanding officer, Major (now Colonel retired) Cornell Westwood. He is unaware of my contacting you as I am sure he would disapprove of it as a waste of your time. However, I am convinced that a man who returned from the Boer War, claiming to be my brother, is an imposter.

While he resembles Charles in his physical build, his face is so scarred that it no longer can confirm his identity. His memory regarding family matters is inaccurate, which he explains is caused by the concussion he received in the same explosion which burned away much of his face. He seems to have some knowledge of events or items of which only Charles should know, and this has convinced my father of his identity. I, however, am less sure. When I look into his eyes or mention a secret that only we shared, he is like an empty shell. I believe that he may have served with my brother and had learned some knowledge of our family, and that he is now using that knowledge with the intention of getting *access to our family fortune. I realise that this implies that my brother must be dead and that this wounded man has taken his place. That saddens me even more than this imposter's tricks sicken me. But I cannot let father be deceived in this way.*

Could you, and hopefully your friend, Mr. Sherlock Holmes, come to Ramsgate and call upon my father and see if I am right?

Yours sincerely,

Victoria Westwood

I let my left hand with the letter drop into my lap as I reached for the sherry sitting on the side table. I recalled the family photograph Westwood kept on his desk of himself, his wife and his two-year-old son, Charles. After my wounds at Maiwand removed me from Her Majesty's service for good, I had heard little news of him. Thus I was unaware of the addition of this daughter, Victoria, to his brood.

"So, Watson," interjected Holmes with such bravado that he startled me from my thoughts. "Is your fiancée aware of this penchant you have for rescuing damsels in distress?"

I straightened up in my chair and held the letter to my chest, "Explain yourself, Holmes!" I demanded, having gone through this little game of his all too often.

"The letter in your hand bears a woman's handwriting, and not that of your fiancée. Your reaction indicates that she, or someone close to her, is in need of assistance, and the faraway look upon your face indicates that you have cast your memory back many years. However, I can tell, even from here, that the handwriting is of a young and strong female who could not have been more than a child, if she was even born, at the time to which your memory has retreated. It is likely, therefore, that she is writing on behalf of one of your old acquaintances, of which you have few, or perhaps a comrade in arms, of which you have many. Judging by her age I would presume that to be a fellow army compatriot or, more likely, a superior officer who is a little older than yourself."

"Do you have to be right all of the time?" I asked in exasperation at having my thoughts read yet again.

"My dear Doctor, you are quite aware of how often I am wrong. You just never include those instances in your little entertainments for the masses."

"Those 'entertainments' have paid for my share of the rent more often than you know. It isn't easy to maintain a thriving practice when I'm off saving the world with you, you know."

"I do know," he replied. "Which is why I consented to let you write up the Baskerville case[1]. How is that going by the way?"

I relaxed somewhat and smiled, "Sales of *The Strand Magazine* have soared since the first instalment in August. Doyle and Smith are quite pleased[2]."

Holmes nodded. As much as he complained, I knew his ego was always pleased to have his name bandied about as the world's greatest consulting detective. Then he continued his query.

"So who has written to you and what assistance is she seeking?"

I handed the letter across to him, stating that it was from the daughter of my former commanding officer at the army hospital in Afghanistan. He perused it quickly mumbling about 'intelligence', 'strength of character' and 'genuine concern' as he automatically judged the handwriting.

---

[1] *The Hound of the Baskervilles* would be the first Holmes story published since 1893.
[2] Arthur Conan Doyle was Dr. Watson's agent and Herbert Greenhough Smith was the magazine's editor.

He handed it back and asked, "She poses a most interesting hypothesis and is convinced that she is right. Will you go down to Ramsgate?"

"There is only so much I can do from a medical standpoint," I replied. "I doubt my opinion would count heavily against Colonel Westwood's belief in this man being his son. 'The heart wants what it wants' to quote Emily Dickinson, and evidence would have to be overwhelming to deter it. It would be more beneficial if you could add your opinion along with any proof you uncover."

Holmes took another pull on his pipe as he took a moment to reply. When he did so I was a little surprised by his answer. "I believe that this is a case where I must remain incognito for the time being, Doctor. If his daughter has expressed her concerns to him and met with obstinance, then the arrival of the two of us will incline him towards putting up more blockades. It will be better if you go yourself, perhaps on the pretext that you are coming down that way on business or holiday and wish to drop in for old-time's sake. I shall also travel to Ramsgate, but make my investigations from the outside. We can communicate by meeting at a local public house or the beach and take further steps from what we find out."

Chapter Two

I wrote to Colonel Westwood that very day, asking if I might call upon him while I was in Ramsgate on a fishing holiday. I received his reply the next afternoon, advising that not only could I visit, but he insisted that I stay with him while in the town.

This suited our purposes perfectly. The Westwood home was less than a ten-minute walk from the Royal Harbour where I could maintain my fiction of coming down for the fishing. Holmes was able to make reservations under his 'Captain Basil'[1] pseudonym at The Falstaff, a local inn, which was right on the sea front close to the pier, so we could meet daily without arousing suspicion. I wrote back to the Colonel advising him that I would come down on Friday, giving him two days to prepare for my arrival, and the appearance that my trip was a leisurely one with no underlying purpose.

Holmes and I spent the time investigating the service records of Colonel Westwood and his son, Charles. As an army pensioner myself, I was able to use my contacts to gain information about Charles's debilitating incident and medical condition.

It transpired that Lieutenant Charles Westwood was on patrol with a platoon of men near Middelburg in the Transvaal

---

[1] Watson would mention Holmes's character of Captain Basil again in the story of *The Adventure of Black Peter* which was published in 1904 in *The Strand Magazine*.

in late May 1901. He had assigned Sergeant Warren Preston to the front with the others following in pairs some way behind. Westwood was closest to Preston on his right when the Sergeant stepped on a land mine. Preston was killed instantly. The concussion and shrapnel blew back upon Westwood and Lance Corporal William Myers to his left and they took the brunt of the explosion. Behind them, others received only minor cuts and bruises. Westwood and Myers were taken to the field hospital where they were treated. Then they were sent to Bloemfontein in the Orange Free State which has the largest hospital in South Africa.

Westwood spent ten weeks there, undergoing surgeries and rehabilitation to his face, arm and hip. There was also damage to his vocal cords, but he was in speech therapy and could maintain conversations for short periods. He had been discharged and was now back at his father's house for just over three weeks.

A photograph of him in uniform before the injury was attached. Charles was a handsome lad full of promise. How his injury might affect his future was a thought I dared not contemplate.

Holmes had been able to gain more than a superficial look at Colonel Westwood's military record since Maiwand. After Afghanistan, Major Westwood was promoted to Colonel and given the supervision of several hospitals during the Mahdist war in the Sudan between 1881 to 1899. He served with distinction, receiving several mentions in dispatches.

When that war ended he retired to the family home in Ramsgate. Unfortunately, it was only months before his wife succumbed to consumption, leaving him with a teenage daughter and to see his son graduate from Sandhurst before being sent off to another British war in Africa.

Armed with these facts by Friday morning, we left London bound for Ramsgate Harbour station and were there in just under two hours.

Chapter Three

During that trip, I read from a book I had picked up at the library so that I might learn a little about the town. There was much regarding the local fishing industry, the excellent beaches, and the famous architecture in the area, and also the fortifications which gave me a background which I felt might be helpful in discussions with a military-minded man such as Colonel Westwood.

Across from me sat Holmes as Captain Basil. He wore only a moustache and goatee beard to hide his features which the artist Sidney Paget had often provided alongside my stories in *The Strand Magazine*. Those illustrations were not particularly accurate regarding Holmes's face or hairline. This was a condition the detective had insisted upon, to hopefully avoid being recognised and stopped continually on the street by admirers, or those seeking his assistance. But his general build as to height and weight were within acceptable margins. As he was never photographed, or written about with facial hair, he felt this affectation would be sufficient to maintain his alternative identity.

Upon our arrival, Holmes insisted that I exit first and he would wait several minutes, so we would not be spotted together. It was well he did so, as Colonel Westwood had chosen to meet me in person on the platform. Fortunately, he recognised me. I had never seen him out of uniform and would never have taken this bald-headed, stout-figured gentleman for the Major I knew with his flowing brown locks and athletic build. The only thing in common with the man I served under was his thick moustache, but even it was now as grey as the fringe of hair left upon his head.

"Watson, dear fellow! Welcome to Ramsgate," he said, pumping my hand in greeting. "Why, you've hardly changed at all, except for adding some weight. I wish I could say the same." He patted his ample stomach and ran his hand over his bald head.

His good humour was infectious and I could not help but smile at him. "Civilian life has been kind to me, sir. I imagine all those years on the battlefield for Queen and country would take their toll on any man. But you look healthy and happy and that is worth everything."

"Well 'healthy' is a relative term. I can't seem to shake this infernal congestion that came on with last summer's allergy season!" he said, patting his chest and clearing his throat. "But come, let's get your luggage and fishing gear and have you settle in so you can relax before lunch." He had a servant with him, one of his former orderlies as it turned out, and we were soon in his coach *en route* to Westwood House. The Colonel's home was a three-storey affair of light grey brick less than half-a-mile from the station. It was across the street from Vale Square Gardens and had a small garden of its own in front, and a mews off to one side for the horse and coach.

As we disembarked, he pointed off to the southeast, "If you want to get in some fishing, your best bet would be straight down Vale Square then jig to the right and turn down Addington for a quarter mile. Then turn left to the harbour where you can find daily fishing charters."

Suddenly his countenance grew serious and he touched my arm, "Before we go inside, I must warn you that my son, Charles, has recently returned from the war in South Africa. He was horribly wounded and his appearance is not a pleasant sight to behold. I ask that you would be sensitive to that."

"I am sorry to hear that, Colonel. I was exposed to many such individuals during my convalescence, and I know what a terrible mental toll it has in addition to the physical injuries. I will act accordingly."

"Thank you, Watson. Let's go in."

The first person to greet us as we entered was a charming young girl who could not have been more than twenty. Her heart-shaped face was framed by long brown curls cascading down her shoulders to her breast. Doe-like, tawny eyes sought mine and portrayed thankfulness at my arrival.

"Dr. John Watson, allow me to introduce my daughter, Victoria. Victoria, Watson was a colleague of mine in Afghanistan back in the late 70s. He's come down on a fishing holiday and will be staying with us for a few days."

She held out her hand which exhibited the long fingers of a musician. I bowed over it politely and said, "I am charmed to meet you, Miss."

"And I you, Doctor," she replied. "Where have you come from?"

She was playing her role perfectly and I replied in kind, "I have a practice in London, but felt a need to get away for a few days. My summer was quite busy and even doctors need a chance to rest occasionally."

"Well, I hope you will enjoy your stay with us then. Ramsgate is a wonderful town to live in and you've come just when the crowds have thinned out, so fishing should be pleasant."

"I am sure I will enjoy it very much," I replied.

"Let's retire to the drawing room for some refreshment while Riggs takes your luggage to your room," said the retired Colonel. "I'll introduce you to my son, Charles."

Chapter Four

Even though Victoria's letter and the Colonel's warning had prepared me for Charles's condition, my first sight of him gave me pause. The young man was seated by a window that looked out upon the greenery of the square. He turned at the sound of our approach and pushed himself up painstakingly from his chair. Leaning heavily on his cane he limped forward and held out his hand, "You must be Dr. Watson. I am pleased to meet you, sir."

I took his hand carefully for it was quite scarred, but he gave me a firm grip indicating that the muscles had healed underneath that wrinkled and warped flesh. A black patch over his right eye was only a slight distraction from the wrinkled pink and white checked skin that covered the right side of his face from his chin to his hairline. But his attitude sought no sympathy. It was, rather, the bravado of a man who accepted his fate and was making the best of it.

After shaking his hand, I was waved towards a seat by the Colonel and took it gratefully. I had been exposed to severely wounded men while in the army, including amputees, and it was only my experiences as a doctor that kept my emotions muted at this pitiable sight. This once handsome young man was now physically scarred for life. I could only imagine the emotional toll it must be taking upon him. Indeed, I wondered if that realisation had fully manifested itself in him yet.

The Colonel had also sat down but Victoria left us to retrieve refreshments from the kitchen. I wasn't sure what to say but Charles solved that problem by asking me questions.

"My father tells me that you were also wounded while in service and I see that you still have a bit of a limp. Were you laid up for very long?"

While I don't relish speaking of my wounding and convalescence, I was grateful for the opportunity to speak without awkwardness. "It was quite some time," I replied. "But that was due to the fact that, while I was recovering from the surgeries that treated my wounds, I came down with enteric fever. I was originally wounded in the shoulder near the subclavian artery while loading up patients for our retreat from Maiwand. Murray, my orderly, helped me onto a pack horse and while he led me out with the troops, a jezail bullet grazed my leg. The shoulder healed quickly, but the leg took longer and still acts up in cold weather. It's become more bearable over time, but now that I am approaching fifty it occasionally decides to remind me that I am no longer a callow youth and I find myself making my rounds via a cab instead of walking them."

"Forgive me, Doctor," said young Westwood. "I am naturally interested in leg wounds and their prognosis. I received wounds both above and below the knee. They tell me that I was lucky in that it missed the femoral artery. They've removed all the shrapnel and they say that only time will tell if the muscles will completely regain their strength. It sounds like yours, though functional, may not have fully recovered. Is that typical?"

I could see that there was both hope and fear in his good eye and I glanced at the Colonel who merely nodded, which I took to mean that I should be truthful. "I cannot make a diagnosis without an examination, x-rays and various other physical tests," I replied. "As I am sure your father has told you, every patient is different and two men with the same injury may respond quite opposite to each other. From my personal experience, I believe that the greatest factor in healing is the mind and attitude of the patient. While it is true that some injuries are impossible to overcome, many can be conquered by sheer determination, or in some cases, complete ignorance."

Charles gave me a quizzical look and I turned to his father and said, "Remember Corporal Gerald?"

Victoria had come back by then and Charles led us all in standing upon her entrance. "Oh, do sit down, please," she said with impatience. "There is no need for such formality in our own house."

Charles responded as he sat, "Forgive me, Victoria."

She just shook her head and served each of us with tea. I repeated my comment about Corporal Gerald and I could see that Colonel Westwood was casting his mind back. "Was he the one with the bad shoulder?"

"Yes," I replied.

He turned to his son with a smile, "Corporal Gordon Gerald, one of our orderlies at Maiwand. Good soldier. Efficient, well-liked, and a walking miracle."

Charles and Victoria both tilted their heads at their father, who continued "One day, I believe it was your Murray who reported it," he said to me. "I was made aware of what appeared to be a serious condition regarding Gerald's health. Apparently, Murray had noticed it while they were dressing, as they shared a common barracks. Gerald's left shoulder appeared to be nothing but skin covering bone on bone. He asked the Corporal if his shoulder hurt and Gerald said 'no', but that it did get fatigued from time to time if he had to do a lot of reaching or lifting with that arm. It took a little convincing, but finally, Gerald reported the condition to Dr. Watson here." He waved to me, indicating that I should pick up the story from there.

"Well, I examined Corporal Gerald and could not believe what I was seeing. To determine what had happened and how he was able to function, I ran him through several tests. He was able to do everything a person with a normal shoulder could do. He could reach in all directions. He could lift a significant amount of weight. He could throw, punch, push and pull with almost the same strength and agility as any right-handed person using his left hand.

"This was unprecedented in my experience. The muscle that normally controls those functions had completely atrophied. It was literally gone, which is why his shoulder looked so skeletal. I called in your father to confirm my results and we were both stumped.

"Then we started asking questions about when he first noticed the change and how did he even pass his army physical. He said that his arm was completely normal when he had joined up two years before. He never really paid much attention to it. He just did his job and used his arm as he normally would. He rarely looked in a mirror without his shirt on, so didn't notice how bad it had gotten until Murray had pointed it out.

"We discussed what we knew about the causes of muscular atrophy, but he was exhibiting no other symptoms. Finally, I suggested neurogenic atrophy. That is a condition where the nerve that controls the muscle becomes injured. We questioned him as to whether he could remember any injury to that shoulder, but he could not. At last, he got tired of our questions and said 'The only time that shoulder ever hurt was when I got my smallpox shot before coming overseas'."

"That was our answer," broke in the Colonel. "We examined his shoulder under a magnifying lens and found the injection site. It was higher up on the arm than it should have been and in exactly the right area where the needle could have severed the nerve."

Victoria shook her head, "But if the muscle was gone, how could he keep using his arm?"

I replied, "That was where ignorance was bliss. He only knew his shoulder was sore from his shot, so he kept using his arm. The human body is a wondrous instrument. Often when one part becomes weak, another takes over. In this case, the other muscles of the arm, back and neck compensated for the weakened shoulder allowing him to keep functioning. He never even realised the adjustments he was making to complete his normal tasks."[1]

---

[1] This incident is based upon an actual occurrence to the author's father, a United States Army sergeant during World War II.

"Did you give him a medical discharge?" asked Charles.

"He wouldn't hear of it," replied his father. "He insisted that he was fine and since he did his work well and was not a frontline soldier, I felt no need to relieve him. I only insisted that he report any deterioration that he could not compensate for and that we would then address it. He served well and remained in the army until he retired."

We finished our tea and I went upstairs to unpack. Victoria sought me out surreptitiously and asked, "Is Mr. Holmes coming with you?"

I replied quietly, "Holmes is in the town and will be investigating, but he did not wish to show up here where his reputation might put your 'brother' on guard, or disturb your father before anything was proven. I presume that your father does not know of my association with Holmes?"

"I don't believe so," she replied.

"Good. Then we will continue to carry on this charade, and while I work from the inside, Holmes will work from the outside and we will see what we may discover between us."

Chapter Five

Lunch was a pleasant affair and our discussions continued with the Colonel sharing some war stories of his career after Maiwand. Despite his handicaps, Charles Westwood carried on as normal as possible. There were hesitations in his speech from time to time, and he would have to turn his head farther than most, in order to look someone that he was talking to in the eye.

I did notice that he seemed to do so less with his sister. This may have been due to his familiarity with her, or perhaps he wished to avoid her scrutiny. At times when he seemed to avoid eye contact she would look in my direction with a twitch or a nod, as if indicating that his action confirmed her suspicion that he was an imposter.

After lunch, I decided to take advantage of the fair weather and indicated that I might go for a walk down to the harbour and look around for a while. The Colonel apologised for not being able to go with me as he had some business to which he needed to attend. Charles offered to drive me as he often takes his Benz Patent-Motorwagen out for a ride since he can no longer walk long distances. The vehicle seats two adults and is hand-controlled, which makes it ideal for his physical limitations, but I cited my need for exercise after the train ride and agreed that we should go out together at some other time.

Of course, my reason for wishing to be alone was to call on Holmes at The Falstaff, an inn about halfway to the harbour on

Addington Street. The building presented a hunter green ground floor façade with the hotel and restaurant entrances separated by a divider. Two upper floors were of used brick. From the street, there was no view of the seafront, though I could see water in the distance, and the smell of the sea was strong as it was but 300 yards from the shore. I spotted Holmes peering out of a white-curtained first-floor bay window trimmed in a darker shade green. He saw me as well and signalled that I should enter.

I walked inside and saw him on the staircase as if he were coming down to go out. For the sake of the desk clerk, he acted surprised to see me and said, "Dr. Watson, is that you?"

"Captain Basil!" I declared as I walked over to him with my arm outstretched for a handshake. "I was just popping in for some refreshment. What are you doing here?"

'Captain Basil' chided me, "You selected the wrong door for the pub I'm afraid. This is the hotel side, but I'm glad to see you. Are you on holiday?"

"Yes, I'm staying with friends nearby. I thought I would explore the harbour and see about some fishing."

"Splendid! Come, let me take you next door and we'll have a round or two."

Once settled in a quiet corner of the pub, Holmes asked me for my report. I told him of the personality change that age and retirement had brought about in my old commander.

"Typical symptoms of old age and reflection upon one's life and legacy," he remarked. "What about the son? Does your medical opinion concur that his injuries could be consistent with memory loss?"

I described the damage and healing progress I had observed and agreed that the concussive blow along with the emotional trauma of seeing the man in front of him blown to pieces was enough to shake any man's memories. But, I also confirmed that I would need more time to observe him, and more information from the sister to make an adequate diagnosis. I advised my friend how Charles was known to go for a drive now and again and described his Benz Patent-Motorwagen that I had seen in the open space next to the house.

Holmes mulled that over, then asked, "Do you know where he goes?"

"I believe that he just likes to get out for some fresh air as it is difficult for him to walk very far, even though there is a nice park right across the street."

Holmes nodded, then suggested, "The next time he offers to drop you off at the harbour, take him up on it, then note which direction he goes afterwards."

"Very well," I replied, then added, "What are you thinking?"

"Nothing specifically," Holmes replied. "It is merely an unknown factor for now and you know my penchant for having exact knowledge."

We finished our ales and I left my friend, continuing my journey to the seafront to explore the various charter craft available for fishing. The sea breeze was invigorating after the smells of London, and I found a spring in my step as I returned to Westwood House in time for tea. The four of us settled into the front room where we had a pleasant enough view of the street and were just being served when a cacophony of squawking arose.

"What on earth is that?" I asked as the crescendo of sound rolled in the window like a tidal wave from the direction of the square across the road.

"Those are our most famous inhabitants," replied Charles with the best effort at a grin he could manage. "The town has a small population of feral rose-ringed parakeets. The story about them appearing in Ramsgate remains a mystery. According to some sources, they may have flown away from the trading ships coming from British India some fifty years ago and thrived here ever since. They have a distinctive green colour with a red beak and a blue tail. They aren't very large, as their wing span is only around a foot. They usually travel in flocks, sometimes as large as fifty birds, and, as you can hear, they are a noisy species, with an unmistakable squawking call. They have taken a particular liking to the trees in the park. If you look out at them you will note that the leaves appear much fuller and greener despite it being autumn. Those are actually the green parakeets resting among the branches before continuing their flight."

In addition to the fascinating fact of this particular species and their migration habit, Charles's statement seemed to indicate to me a confirmation of his identity. It would be odd for a stranger to remember this specific story of Ramsgate. I resolved to pass this fact along to Holmes when next I saw him.

Chapter Six

The next day I continued my ruse and packed up my fishing gear early in the morning, expecting to catch an early boat before breakfast and make it a half-day excursion. I had announced my intention the evening before and Charles offered to drive me to the harbour. I accepted his gracious invitation and also that of Colonel Westwood and his daughter, who said that they would make lunch reservations for us all at The Admiral Harvey pub on York Street. I had hoped to stop by The Falstaff and update Holmes after my fishing trip, but could not very well turn down my host.

Next morning, Charles left me on the quayside of my charter where I joined five other fellows for a morning run out into the Channel. I noted that when he got to the next intersection after dropping me off, he did not turn to go back home, but kept driving north. I made sure I would remember to tell Holmes that fact by noting the word 'north' on a slip of paper in my pocket.

The day was pleasant after the sun's heat finally reached us as it rose in the sky and there was fine camaraderie among the fishermen. I introduced myself merely as John Hamish, not wishing for any recognition of my connection with Holmes and having to spend the day answering endless questions about his adventures, or discussing ailments for those seeking free doctor's advice.

Generally, I am more of a freshwater fisherman, but our guide, a gruff old captain named Kettleman, knew the tides and currents around Ramsgate and where the best fishing was in the mornings. We all were successful in our catch and I managed to reel in some whiting pout and a few cod before we steamed back to port.

Lunch with Colonel Westwood and his children was an agreeable affair. The food at The Admiral Harvey was quite excellent and our table offered a view of the harbour with its many craft going in and out. I asked the Colonel if he went fishing much and he replied that he used to, but his sea legs were not what they used to be and he now confined his fishing to the pier. His next statement intrigued me though.

"Charles and I used to go out on the sea when I would come home on leave. Those were some of our best times. When Victoria was old enough she would join us as well. I've suggested that the two of them should renew their fishing adventures, but apparently, when a lady reaches a certain age it is no longer seemly."

Victoria disputed that remark, "I would gladly set aside any issues of decorum if Charles would go with me." I read from her tone that she refused to take the blame for her brother's lack of interest in fishing.

Charles answered, "It's not for lack of wanting your company, Vicky. I assure you that I would be glad for it. But between my leg wound and the equilibrium problems I have been left with from my concussion, I'm afraid that trying to stand on a pitching deck is out of the question."

She slipped me an unobtrusive look, then said, "We could still bring chairs and sit on the pier to fish from there with father."

Charles seemed to pause before answering, then replied, "Perhaps when I am stronger."

I had noted some slight hesitation when Charles had called his sister 'Vicky' instead of 'Victoria'. It may have meant nothing and just been a result of his throat injury, but I still made a mental note of it. Our conversation turned to other things, then we returned to Westwood House where the

Colonel and I engaged in a few rounds of chess as we discussed old comrades in arms. When it came time for tea, I explained that I needed to stretch my legs after hours of sitting at the chess table and offered to assist Victoria in the kitchen.

Once alone she asked again what my thoughts were regarding this man who claimed to be her brother. I was forced to reply that I had yet to see or hear any evidence that could not be explained by his injuries.

She shook her head, "With father gone so much Charles and I were inseparable growing up. His hesitation to go fishing with me is totally out of character. Those were some of our best times."

I nodded, then asked the question that had been on my mind, "Does Charles go for drives often?"

"Yes, several times a week. Daily, if the weather is good."

"Do you know where he goes?"

"No. I've offered to keep him company but he says he just likes to be alone to think and meditate."

"Could he be visiting someone? A woman, perhaps?"

Victoria gasped at that and her face took on a puzzled expression, "I … I never even thought of that. He had no special female friend before he went off to war. With his injuries …" She stopped, not wishing to appear judgmental of his scarred appearance and its likely influence against female attraction.

I rescued her from her conundrum by suggesting, "Some men fall in love with their nurses. And some nurses take pity upon their patients and look past the body and into the heart. I've seen it often. Especially among soldiers who have been away from feminine company for a long time."

She nodded, then said, "But that doesn't explain his forgetfulness or the lack of skills he grew up with. Did father happen to mention that Charles used to beat him at chess more often than not, and now can't seem to remember the basic strategies of the game?"

"Hmm, that is odd," I replied. "It could be a result of the concussion, but it is telling all the same." She asked about Holmes and I told her my plan to next see him. She suggested an alternative and it seemed reasonable enough for me to agree.

Chapter Seven

Holmes has often accused me of being too accommodating to a pretty face and I admit that Victoria Westwood was indeed such a charmer. However, I was engaged and she was also young enough to be my daughter, so her request seemed perfectly reasonable since she was, after all, our client.

After tea, I mentioned that I had lost one of my favourite lures that morning and intended to go into town to replace it and perhaps do some shopping before dinner. Victoria asked if she could accompany me and, with her father's permission for me to be her chaperone, we set off for an enjoyable walk.

Upon reaching The Falstaff, we entered the hotel side. The desk clerk gave a wary look at me and my young female companion, but seemed satisfied when I asked if Captain Basil was in. A page boy was sent to fetch him and soon the tall gaunt figure of a seafaring man came tromping down the stairs. He did not hesitate when he saw me in the company of Miss Westwood but merely suggested that we drop into the pub next door for some refreshment.

When seated I introduced 'Captain Basil' to our client and she readily fell into the plot by referring to him by that name. "I am quite pleased to meet you, Miss Westwood," he stated. "While Watson is as true and faithful a companion as one could wish for, nothing beats the knowledge of first-hand observers who are at the heart of the matter."

"First," said I, "let me report what you asked for. After dropping me off at the harbour this morning, Charles did not immediately return to the house, but instead, continued up Royal Parade Road to the north."

"It's true, Mr … Captain," said the young lady. "Charles did not return to the house for over two hours after he left with Dr. Watson. His drives usually last about two or three hours and he goes out nearly every day when the weather is fine."

Holmes continued to question Miss Westwood for information. Among those questions were whether or not there were items in the house which might have Charles's fingerprints from before he left. Unfortunately, everything had been cleaned in anticipation of his return and she could think of nothing for comparison. I had to admit that she was a remarkably observant and intelligent girl. A credit to her parents and she might, were she a man, have made a fine officer herself.[1]

We left Holmes and finished our shopping expedition with a new fishing lure for me and a new Irish Donegal tweed bucket hat for her. As she picked it out I commented, "It is hardly a high society fashion for a young lady such as yourself."

She smiled as she put it on her head and gazed into a mirror, "No, Doctor, but it is exactly the fashion for my personality. You see, I'm more tomboy than debutante. Which, I suppose, is another reason why I miss the man my brother used to be. We did everything together. That's why I can't believe this is the same man. He treats me like a lady instead of the sister he used to wrestle and climb trees with."

"That sounds more like that he's matured and is showing you the respect that your station deserves."

Her expression grew hard and for a brief moment, I saw the face of the major I served under in Maiwand. Then she expounded, "Station be hanged! I'm still the same person. Certainly, I like pretty things and dressing up occasionally. But

---

[1] It wasn't until the 1st World War that British women were formally allowed to serve in any capacity other than nursing. They were not allowed in combat roles until 1991-92 in Northern Ireland.

I'll not turn into one of those simpering helpless women with their scheming feminine whiles who look to trap a man instead of having him love them for who they truly are!"

I have had enough experience of women to know when to keep quiet so I let the matter drop. She finished her purchase and we walked home, arriving just before sunset. When we walked in and saw Charles she decided to test him by wearing her new hat and playfully asking, "What do you think, Chucky?"

The former Lieutenant sat, seemingly dumbfounded for a moment. I wondered if it was surprise at the use of his nickname. Then a look came into his eye that I could not discern, but appeared to express some strong emotion. A smile came to his face, however, and he replied, "Absolutely stunning, dear. It's perfect for you."

This was not the answer she was expecting. She bowed her head in confusion, her brow furrowing as she removed the hat, and merely said, "Thank you", then proceeded upstairs to her room.

I noticed Charles's eyes follow her, and then he turned to me, "Did you find a good lure, Doctor?"

I pulled my purchase from my pocket and showed it to him. "That is a beauty," he commented. "I may have to buck up and see about getting down to the pier again."

"It would be good upper body exercise for you," I replied as my medical opinion was always at the ready.

"I'll see," he answered. Then he hesitantly asked, "If I may be so bold, Dr. Watson, what do you think of my sister?"

Not quite sure what he was implying, I asked warily, "I don't take your meaning, sir."

He must have realised my concern and stammered to put my mind at ease, "I ... I didn't mean to cast aspersions, Doctor. I only meant ... well, she has grown into a beautiful woman but I don't think she realises it. Do you think this 'tomboy' personality of hers will be disadvantageous in her ability to marry well?"

I eased my guard and smiled at him, "I think that she is a breath of fresh air. There is nothing phoney about her. That,

Lieutenant, is an excellent quality for a woman to have. Were I a much younger and unengaged man, I would take her ten times over most of the society maidens who debut every year."

"Well, I hope she finds a worthy man of her age who thinks like you," he replied.

I studied him momentarily, then asked, "Why this concern over her future, Charles?"

He hesitated, then replied, in a somewhat forced manner I thought, "It's just that … father is getting older and if something happens to him before she gets married I would not want her future to be affected by some suitor thinking that he would have to have me as a burden under her care."

I thought this an odd remark but then he changed the subject and offered me a drink and a game of chess. "I need the practice," he said. "I've not been able to give father the challenge I used to."

I acquiesced but made a mental note to report this conversation to Holmes when next I saw him.

Chapter Eight

In the morning I prepared for another half-day fishing trip, and once more, Charles offered to drive me to the harbour. This time I advised the Colonel that I would be coming home for lunch, but there was no need to pick me up as I was not sure when we would return. This ploy would allow me to stop by The Falstaff and speak with Holmes again.

As we boarded Charles's machine, I noticed a horse and trap down the street. The driver had gotten out and was checking the horse's right foreleg. I recognised that it was Holmes, keeping an eye out for us leaving so that he could follow and see just where our young friend was going on his excursions. I therefore engaged the lad in conversation and stood where his good eye would not be looking in Holmes's direction.

The contraption had a top speed of ten miles per hour, but Westwood never accelerated to full throttle while driving me around town. He felt it was too dangerous for pedestrians and horse-drawn vehicles to react to such speed if we came upon them unawares. Thus he kept his pace to about five miles per hour, which I knew Holmes and his horse could match over short distances.

The fishing expedition went about the same as my previous one, I had some success, but nothing to brag about. When I reached The Falstaff on the way home, I met with Holmes in his room where he was smoking his pipe. Evidently, he had been doing so and meditating on the case for some time as there was a thick blue haze in the room.

Full of curiosity I asked, "Well, where did young Charles go after he dropped me off?"

Holmes grunted then remarked, "He almost lost me once he got north of the harbour. He felt safer at full speed after he left the town centre and was traversing the quiet residential streets towards Dumpton Park. I was just able to keep his vehicle in sight until he stopped in front of the Holy Trinity Convalescent Centre. There was a large grassy area across the street, so I pulled around the corner where I could see over the flat ground to the front gate in the hedge surrounding the building. He stayed just under an hour, then got onto his vehicle and returned home."

"So what will you do next?"

"Tomorrow I will visit there in the guise of a doctor, if I may borrow a couple of your business cards, Watson."

I handed two of them over to him and he set them on the table. "I shall pretend to be doing a study on wounded soldiers for the Foreign Office. Hopefully, I shall be able to ascertain why Lieutenant Westwood is going there."

He then changed the subject, "I did observe something today which I would like you to confirm for me, Watson."

"Certainly, if I can," I replied.

Holmes asked, "With your military experience, would you agree that an officer leading a column of twos would be at the head of the right-hand column so that he could signal to all of his men silently with his left hand while his weapon was in his right?"

I nodded, "Yes, that would be standard practice. And the reports I saw of the incident indicated that Westwood was at the head of the right column when the man to his left stepped on the land mine. Why?"

"I observed that Westwood's injuries were all to his right side, agreed?"

"Of course, Holmes. Charles is right-handed. The natural instinct would be for him to throw up his right hand to protect his face which would cause his body to turn to the left, exposing his right side, which is where all of his serious injuries occurred. What are you suggesting?" I asked with narrowed eyes.

"Just ensuring facts before I delve into a rabbit hole," he replied, enigmatically, then asked, "Have you any other developments to report?"

I reiterated the actions and conversation of the previous day's encounter between Victoria and her brother, and how his demeanour seemed odd. "It was strange, Holmes. The Colonel's health seems fine other than his occasional coughing fits, and Victoria's beauty, despite her outspoken ways, will attract many a suitor. I believe that she will be able to take her pick. Charles is certainly no invalid who needs her care and I would imagine that he could live quite comfortably on his inheritance and army pension when the time comes. He has no reason to expect to be a burden on her or a detractor from any potential suitors."

Holmes puffed at his pipe, then replied, "That is very interesting. How was his chess game?"

"Adequate, but certainly not advanced. The level of play he exhibited to me would be no match for his father. I played Westwood several times when we served and he is excellent. I could give him a run for his money, though I believe that I only beat him once. I would put him at a level similar to yours."

I must confess to the reader that I had given up playing chess against Holmes within the first year of our lodging together. The man seemed able to predict my every move, while he used gambits that appeared totally illogical until you suddenly found yourself checkmated.

"Could his injuries explain his declined skills, Doctor?" queried Holmes.

I squinted as I tilted my head, "Possible, but I shouldn't think likely. In all other cognitive functions, he seems quite fine. I suppose that his concussion could account for the diminished chess skills, but selective memory loss is impossible to predict."

"Well we shall see," said Holmes. "You keep an eye on him and I will investigate the convalescent centre tomorrow. I've also wired to London for further information regarding a hypothesis that I am considering."

"Which is?"

He shook his head, "You know me better than that, Watson. When I have enough facts for a reasonable conclusion I shall share it. In the meantime, I do not wish to prejudice your observations with a theory which may prove erroneous."

Chapter Nine

I returned to Westwood House by 1.15 p.m. and was served a late lunch which I shared with the Colonel, who was kind enough to wait for me. As we ate I brought up the subject of the chess games I had played with Charles the night before.

"I understand that he used to be able to give you a fair match. I was surprised that his injuries have affected his skills."

Westwood pursed his lips, "Yes, it is a shame how war can rob one of the vibrancy of their lives. Charles was a brilliant lad. I expected that he would have risen high in the ranks, possibly to a general. He was of the new breed of officer; those young bucks who see their men as men and not just as numbers to throw at the enemy. It makes them more cautious, which means that they consider multiple options in their tactics. Those are the officers who will win our future wars."

I raised my wineglass, "Let us hope the next generation can find alternatives to war."

Westwood echoed my toast and we went on to discuss other things. One item we agreed to was his suggestion that we go fishing together from the pier the next morning. This would curtail my contacting Holmes, but I could not refuse his invitation.

Later that afternoon, Victoria, wearing her new hat, announced that she wished to go for a walk in the garden square across the road and asked if I would join her. I took up my cane, donned my Panama hat, and we set out for a leisurely stroll. Once across the street and out of earshot of the house, she began her questions.

"Was Mr. Holmes able to follow Charles this morning? Where did he go?"

Gazing about to see that no one else was nearby, I replied, "Your brother went to the Holy Trinity Convalescent Centre in Dumpton Park. He stayed about a half an hour then left."

"What do you suppose he was doing there?" she asked, with a quizzical look.

"That would be sheer conjecture at this point. It could possibly be a therapy session, or he may have been visiting someone. Holmes intends to infiltrate there tomorrow and learn what he may."

We walked on a few more steps having almost reached the far end of the gardens. Miss Westwood seemed lost in thought as we turned to go back. Finally, she looked up at me and asked, "Could you have been right about his falling in love with a nurse?"

She had a strange look upon her face when she asked the question. If the man was truly not her brother, I might have put it down to jealousy. I decided discretion, rather than speculation, was in order.

"I would rather wait for the results of Holmes reconnoitring tomorrow rather than hazard a guess at this juncture." Then I stopped and looked down into that concerned face, "If he has fallen in love, would that upset you?"

She shook her head quickly, "Oh … no, no. If that is the case and it truly is Charles, I would be quite happy that he has found someone willing to overlook his injuries."

I ignored the emotion she seemed to be hiding and replied, "It might also explain his changed attitude towards you. He could be seeing women differently if he has fallen in love with one, and is treating you with that same new-found respect for ladies since you have become one yourself … despite your insistence at being a tomboy."

I grinned at this last remark and she could not help but laugh. Soon her laughter was drowned out by the squawking parrots in the trees between us and Westwood House and we found that we could no longer carry on a conversation over that loud clamour while traversing those last few yards.

We entered the house in good humour, relieved at being able to shut the door against the deafening noise. Charles limped into the entrance hall and asked how we had enjoyed our walk, but there was an edge to his voice that belied the smile on his face.

Victoria, trying too hard to cover for our true discussion, blurted out, "Dr. Watson is an excellent conversationalist for a man of his age. He understands the finer points of tree climbing and was apparently quite adept at it in his younger days. Do you remember the fun we used to have climbing those trees in the square and spying on the neighbours, Chucky?"

He looked at her askance and replied, "Don't you think it's time to put away childish things, Victoria? Reminiscences of skinned knees and scraped knuckles are hardly the topics in which a young woman should be indulging."

At this point I could see that there were harsh emotions in both their eyes and felt that I should step in before one or the other said something regretful. "Children …" I exclaimed, bringing both of them up short as they turned their sharp eyes upon me, thinking I was addressing them as such. I continued, "… are the treasure of civilisation. Even adults who do not have children recognise that they are the future of society."

I looked directly at Charles, "They are among the reasons we fight wars. So they might enjoy peace when they grow up." Turning to Victoria I continued, "They are the reason we create inventions and study medicine; to make their lives better than ours."

I put my hands on my hips and gave them a stern look, "So many adults do not have happy childhood memories. Those who do *should* rejoice in them. I'm not saying to keep living in the past. But I implore you as strongly as I can, treasure the memories of it. They may be the happiest times of your life."

They had the good sense to calm down and so, just to satisfy my curiosity, I gave one more order, "Now hug each other and say you're sorry."

Charles started to protest until I said, "I outrank you, Lieutenant. Now that's an order." Despite the fact that we had both been discharged from service due to our injuries, it was still hard for the younger man to disregard an elder, so he turned towards his sister.

The look of discomfort on both their faces seemed to confirm my suspicions. Reluctantly they approached each other and gave as chaste and comradely a hug as a brother and sister should. It lasted as briefly as possible and they looked quickly away from each other and towards me as they separated.

"That's better," I said, glancing at my watch "Now, tea time."

Chapter Ten

I believed that I should report my recent observations and conversation to Holmes, as they might be useful to him. However, I could think of no way to communicate with him until at least after my fishing expedition with Colonel Westwood.

As I sat in my room later that night, digesting all that I had seen and heard, an idea struck me as to how I could relay it to the detective. I took up pencil and paper and wrote out my report. I sealed it in an envelope and addressed it to 'Captain Basil, Falstaff Inn'. The next morning, I told the Colonel that I would like to drop it off on our way to the pier. I explained that it was some advice for a fellow fisherman I had met on my earlier excursion and it regarded a medical condition of which he had complained.

Of course, Captain Basil was not in, when we arrived, and as I had suspected that he would want to be at the medical facility at the same time as Charles usually visited. However, it would be waiting for him when he returned, and I hoped it would supplement whatever other information he had gained on that day.

Westwood and I had taken some folding chairs with us and set them up in the cul-de-sac on the end of the pier. We had a pleasant time speaking of old comrades and current politics in between reeling in a few fish. Surprisingly, after a time, we were joined by Charles. He had driven out as far as the road would take him, then limped along the last hundred feet of walkway to where we sat. The Colonel was very pleased to see him and, as a doctor, I felt it was just the sort of activity to assist with his recovery. I offered him my pole and took myself back to where there were some benches, about twenty feet back from the railings. He tried to turn me down but I insisted and he sunk into the chair I had vacated next to his father.

I could still hear their conversation from where I sat and it seemed to reinforce Charles's identity as he talked of past fishing trips and incidents that had happened during them. On the other hand, the rapidity with which he recounted these adventures almost seemed as if he was repeating something he had learned, and wanted to get it out before he forgot the details. If it raised any suspicions to the Colonel he did not react to it.

As noon approached we chose to call it a day and packed up our catch and gear. The Colonel and I returned to the house in the trap while Charles drove his vehicle slowly so that we might all arrive together. When we walked in, we were in good spirits, but Victoria frowned and greeted her brother with "Where have you been? You're never gone this long! I thought that you had had an accident!"

Charles tried to calm her down, "I found myself near the pier while I was driving and decided to join father and Dr. Watson for a while. I only meant to see how they were doing, but the Doctor insisted that I take his pole and get some exercise."

He turned to me and added, "I admit that your prescription was quite invigorating, Doctor. Thank you."

Victoria, seemingly embarrassed by her reaction, calmed down and said, "I'm sorry, brother. I just worry about you."

This seemed to take the Lieutenant off guard though he tried to shake it off with a grin and commented to me, "Fourteen months I'm gone off to war and now she worries about me on the streets of my own city."

She gave him a slap on the shoulder and cried, "You know what I mean. Your ..." She stopped, realising that she was about to comment on his condition and not wishing to make him think that she thought him incapable of taking care of himself. She finished weakly with, "I just wish you had told me. Or better yet, come home and gotten me to come along too!"

"Very well, Sis., I'll try to remember. For now, how about helping me clean up these fish for our supper?"

The siblings went off while the Colonel and I settled down for some lunch to ourselves. Looking to me he said, "Thank you, Watson. I've longed to see the day when Charles returned to such activities. It's a big step."

"Anyone who has been through such trauma needs to return to as normal a life as he can as quickly as possible," I replied. "People handle their feelings at different rates, and it is not good to rush them, but getting stuck in their grief isn't good either. I'm glad to see this progress for the lad."

Just after two o'clock, a messenger arrived with a letter for me. I broke the seal and read, 'Dear Dr. Watson – Unexpected side effect to the medicine you prescribed. Will you please come to consult at 4.00 p.m.? – Captain Basil, Falstaff Inn'.

I left in good time to make this appointment, taking my medical bag to maintain the ruse. I was anxious to learn where Holmes's investigation had led. Again, for privacy's sake, we met in his room. There was a small table with two chairs, but he kept pacing the floor while I sat. The blue haze had not cleared from the previous day and by this, I could only surmise that he had entered into another deep meditation.

Finally, after a minute, he stopped and said, "Charge your pipe, Watson, we have some deep thinking to do."

I took this to mean that he had made a significant discovery, but that it was one of those cases where he needed me as a sounding board. I lit my amber-stemmed briar and prepared to absorb whatever information he had to impart.

"You asked me why I was inquiring about the formation of Westwood's column. Your supposition of the facts and their interpretation, on the surface, seemed reasonable, no doubt. However, not being a military man and looking at the event from a purely logical standpoint, I came to a different conclusion. With the information I learned today, my hypothesis has proven correct."

"Which is?"

He sat down and addressed me most seriously, "Your view of the incident is that Westwood turned away from the blast to his left, exposing his right side to the injuries he suffered."

"It is a logical conclusion and explains the result," I agreed.

Holmes bit his lip and slowly shook his head, "That would presume that he had a split second's warning, in which case he would have ducked as he turned and had at least some lacerations to his back. Also, raising his hand up to protect his face should have reduced his eye and facial injuries, but they appear to have taken the full force of the blast without hindrance."

"You have another explanation?" I queried.

Holmes sat back, his hands folded in front of him. "I believe that the blast was instantaneous and that this gentleman's injuries are the result of his inability to perceive the danger until it literally, hit him in the face. If that is the case, then the natural supposition would be that he was to the rear and *left* of the explosion. That would account for the many injuries to his right side."

I shook my head at his surmise, but then gave him a start, "But that would mean that either Charles was in the wrong formation or this man is ..."

"Lance Corporal William Myers," finished Holmes.

Chapter Eleven

While I digested that conclusion, Holmes lit his own pipe, crossed one knee over the other and waited.

At last, I found my voice, "It holds together as you state it, but have you any other proof that would satisfy the Colonel?"

In reply, he picked up an envelope which had lain off to the side of the table. "I received this in response to my enquiry." He pulled a photograph from it and slid it across to me. "Recognise anyone?"

It only took a quick glance, "That fellow on the right looks like Charles," I answered. Then I looked at the back. There were three names listed and the third was William Myers.

I slid the photograph back to him, "Admittedly they look enough alike that any difference could be explained by their injuries," I countered. "But how could Myers know all the personal information about the family, and the house, and the town?"

"There lies the real crux of my problem," said my companion. "The reason for Myer's visits to the convalescent centre is to see a patient. The patient's name is listed as William Myers. But I got a look at him today and his injuries are similar to *your* Charles Westwood's, except that they are to the opposite side of his face and body, which supports my theory that he is Westwood and his left side received the brunt of the blast. Unfortunately, his wounds are much more serious. His face is horribly scarred, he has lost sight in his left eye, he can only speak with difficulty in a raspy voice and his leg is not wounded, it is gone. They had to amputate it before they sent him home."

"My God!" I cried.

"Therein lies my vexation, Doctor. Obviously, Myers has replaced Westwood at the Lieutenant's request for not wishing to face his family in his pitiable state. The Lieutenant is feeding him the information that he needs to maintain the fiction. The Corporal is not out for sordid gain, but to honour his friend and superior officer. Our client was correct in her suspicions as to his identity, though not to his motive. But is exposing the truth against her brother's wishes the right and proper thing to do?"

Editor's Note

Dear Reader,

I regret to inform you that Dr. Watson's notes on this case end at this point. The rest of the pages are missing, or perhaps accidentally destroyed. With Holmes's question left hanging in the air, the obvious course of action would be to finish the story in some fashion. The historical records are of no help as Ramsgate was a frequent target of bombing in both world wars and many documents were destroyed.

In my consultations with my Holmesian friends, we have not been able to agree on any one solution. Some say 'Holmes must stand for truth above all and expose the scheme to the Colonel'. Others argue that Holmes often, in concert with Watson, acted as his own judge and jury, such as in The Adventure of the Abbey Grange[1] and should not divulge what he learned. Others prefer a compromise – such as informing their client of the truth, and leaving it up to her whether or not she would expose her brother's secret.

All of these scenarios have their pros and cons. Therefore, rather than choose one over the others, the decision will be left up to you. Hence I present three final chapters to the story, each with a different ending and leave it to you to decide for yourself which you prefer.

---

[1] By Arthur Conan Doyle and published in *The Strand Magazine* in September 1904.

Chapter Twelve

The Truth Remains Untold

I sympathised with Holmes's plight. He had a responsibility to his client, however, the real Charles Westwood had his right to privacy. We had maintained our silence in cases before. One case that came to mind was the Milverton murder[1] which we witnessed but did not reveal what we knew to Scotland Yard for our belief that justice had been served.

In this case, no real harm was being done. Rather, a family was being spared the grief of the true knowledge of the soldier's horrific condition. I could certainly make a case for keeping silent. However, such a momentous decision was not to be taken lightly.

"Holmes," I said, "before taking a vow of silence, I should like to see the young man. I know his father and have come to know his sister. I need to speak with him to assure myself that his reasoning is sound for all concerned."

I dashed off a message to Colonel Westwood stating that my patient's condition would require my services for some time and that I may be late for dinner. Then Holmes and I took a cab to the Holy Trinity Convalescent Centre. Fortunately, the dayshift had given way to the night staff and we were able to

---

[1] *The Adventure of Charles Augustus Milverton* by Arthur Conan Doyle and published in *The Strand Magazine* in March 1904.

avoid the confusion of Holmes having used my name previously. We were able to gain permission from Myers's doctor to visit the lad.

Upon entering his room he seemed perturbed at the sight of visitors and turned away from us saying in his raspy voice, "Go away!"

I replied as gently but firmly as possible, "I am afraid that we must speak, Lieutenant Westwood."

Being addressed by his own name seemed to freeze him momentarily. Then, he turned back towards us, stared at us with his good eye, and replied, "You've got the wrong person. I am Lance Corporal William Myers."

I shook my head slowly, "I am Dr. John Watson, formerly of the Fifth Northumberland Fusiliers. I served under your father at the Battle of Maiwand and I am currently visiting him at the suggestion of your sister who does not believe that the man you sent in your place is you."

I turned and indicated my companion, "This is Mr. Sherlock Holmes, the detective. He has determined that you have requested Myers to take your place to spare your family and yourself the pain of your condition becoming known. I need to speak with you regarding whether or not we should keep your secret or confirm your sister's suspicions."

As he sat up in the bed and gazed down at his missing limb. I could see his lips curl in anger. "Why are you butting in?" he shouted at last. "I have everything under control! I give Will the information he needs to maintain his role. He has access to my money so that my bills here are paid. My father is spared the pain of a crippled son, and my sister will not have to take pity on me and ruin her life by caring for me. Just leave it alone!"

I shook my head, "I must confirm that you have thought this through before I make such a decision. Why do you feel it necessary to keep the truth from your father?"

He harrumphed, "If you served with my father then you should know that. As an officer in Her Majesty's service, he disdains anyone with weakness. How do you suppose that he would react to a son with a missing eye, a missing leg, and who can no longer speak in normal tones?"

I thought back to my days of service with, then Major, Westwood. He was a strict commander, but he was no martinet. He expected the absolute best of his men and would certainly discipline those who failed his standards. But he was also a doctor who had great sympathy for the wounded. Certainly, he would drive them hard for their own good to do their exercises and take their treatments. But that was to keep up their morale so that they would not succumb to self-pity and fail to regain whatever potential they had.

I said as much to the Lieutenant, but he replied, "You knew him as a doctor and an officer, Dr. Watson. You have no idea what his expectations as a father were. I never wanted to follow in his footsteps and enter the military. I wanted to be an engineer and design automobiles. That is the future. I saw what a military man's life is like; being away from your family for months or even years at a time. That's not the life I wanted. But you don't say 'no' to Colonel Cornell Westwood."

He had said this last sarcastically, then looked down at his missing leg again and slapped the bed where it should have been. "I couldn't say 'no' and look what it got me! I never want to see that man again! So the two of you can just bugger off and leave me alone!"

Holmes had remained silent during this dialogue, but now spoke up, "What of your sister? She seems determined to expose Myers as a fraud."

That seemed to give Westwood pause, but after a moment he shook his head, "No, Vicky is better off this way. Will's injuries are not so serious as she would feel obligated to take care of him. She can marry and he will soon be well enough to find work and get out from under the Colonel's scrutiny. All will be well and no one the wiser."

Holmes looked to me and I gave a begrudging nod. I took out one of my cards and set it on the table next to the Lieutenant's bed. "Very well. We shall keep your secret. But if you ever change your mind and you wish an intermediary to help soften the blow, here is my card. Feel free to call upon me."

The young man let out a sigh of relief, "Thank you, gentlemen. Trust me, this way is better for all concerned."

That evening, as I was about to retire for the night, I was accosted by Victoria when we happened to be alone at the base of the stairs. She pulled me aside and asked, "Did Mr. Holmes learn anything? Is this man a fraud?"

I had already gone over in my mind what I would tell her and, fortunately, was able to do so with a straight face, "Holmes has found no evidence that your brother is an imposter. He has been visiting a former comrade at the Convalescent Centre as he feels somewhat responsible for his injuries, as any good officer would."

"Really?"

"Yes, my dear. You have no cause for concern. This man will not disappoint your father and you may feel at ease that your brother is exactly where he should be."

Chapter Twelve

The Truth is Revealed to All

I sympathised with Holmes's plight. As he had once told me 'Once or twice in my career I feel that I have done more real harm by my discovery of the criminal than ever he had done by his crime'.[1]

"I see your trouble, Holmes, but if you keep this information to yourself and tell Victoria everything is as it should be, I doubt that she would believe even you. She is bound and determined to prove this man is a fraud, and I think she secretly wishes it to be true."

"How did you come to that conclusion, Doctor?" he asked with great interest.

"I have observed that Myers, as we now know him to be, has been treating Victoria more like a lady than a sister. And he has also exhibited some signs of jealousy. Victoria, in turn, seems to be softening her attitude towards him and appeared envious when I suggested that his long drives in the morning might be to visit a nurse he has fallen in love with."

Holmes tilted his head and blew a puff of smoke towards the ceiling, watching it slowly rise. Then, turning to me, he said, "That certainly speaks in favour of revealing the entire truth. If Myers's identity is not revealed, he certainly cannot court his 'sister' and she, in turn, cannot express her true feelings towards him."

---

[1] *The Adventure of the Abbey Grange* by Arthur Conan Doyle published in The Strand Magazine in September 1904.

"How should we handle it?" I asked.

Holmes laid out a plan and we put it in play the next day.

The following morning I advised the Colonel that I needed to check on my patient but would be home for lunch. After I left, Victoria announced that she was going to visit a friend and asked 'Charles' to drop her off. As they approached the Falstaff Inn, she told him to pull up behind the cab that was out in front. As he did so, Holmes and I stepped out of the cab and walked up on either side of his Motorwagen. She wrapped an arm around his elbow to keep him from attempting to get away. As we approached I announced, "Corporal Myers, your secret is known. If you would please follow us, we are all going to have a discussion with Lieutenant Westwood and see how we might best resolve this situation."

Startled by this revelation, Myers reached to engage the throttle but Victoria's grip was firm. "It's all right, Will," she said, and he could see in her eyes that he had nothing to fear. He relaxed and agreed to follow our cab. As we drove to the Convalescent Centre I could see behind us that the two young people were having a deep conversation. I hoped this meant that my surmises were correct as to their feelings for each other.

When we arrived it took some convincing of the doctor to let all four of us visit 'Lance Corporal Myers' at once, but, with the assurance that I was also a doctor and would keep the situation from escalating to one which might endanger the patient's physical or emotional state, he acquiesced and led us to the room.

Westwood turned at the sound of his door opening and gasped when he saw the four of us standing there. "Wha … what is this? Myers, what have you done?"

"It wasn't me, Lieutenant. Your sister is smarter than you give her credit."

Westwood then turned his attention to the young woman he hadn't seen in over a year. "Vicky? My God, look at you! You're more beautiful than ever."

But as she rushed forward to embrace him he turned away, "No! Don't look at me! Remember the brother you once had.

Not this wretched wreck which I have become. Please go away!"

But she would not leave his side. Though his back was now to her, she held his shoulders, leaned her head into his neck and cried, "It's all right, Chucky. I'm here and everything is going to be all right."

Myers had prepared her for her brother's condition and she bore up to it like a trooper. She sat up straight and said to his back, "You listen to me, Lieutenant Charles Westwood," she said in her most commanding tone. "As soon as the doctor says you are able, you are coming home. I will not have you hide your life away all alone."

"Father will never accept me like this," said Westwood, shaking his head.

"Father is a changed man since retirement and he has certainly accepted Will here, thinking he was you. All he wants is his son back. Your physical condition does not matter. Besides," she grinned, "Will is hopeless at chess and father needs a good match."

Westwood frowned, but Myers tilted his head sheepishly, "I'm afraid she's right Lieutenant. I never was any good at chess."

"And father only goes fishing from the pier now. You could do that from a wheelchair," she added. "Oh, please, Chucky. Come home!"

Finally, Westwood was looking in our direction and asked, "Who are these two gentlemen?"

She pointed to me, "That is Dr. John Watson from father's old regiment at Maiwand, and that is his friend, the detective, Sherlock Holmes."

His head snapped back at his sister and he fixed his good eye upon her, "You called in Sherlock Holmes to find me?"

"As gallant as Mr. Myers has been," she smiled. "I knew he wasn't you. You were never that polite to me. Not to mention his 'memory lapses'. I couldn't call the police without evidence, so I asked Dr. Watson to bring in the world's best detective to find you."

He stared at Holmes and said, "I'm not sure that I should thank you, sir. I had this all worked out. Will has no family so he would be taken care of. I would keep my privacy, Vicky would not have me for a burden, and father would be none the wiser."

Holmes bowed to the young man and replied, "I understand your feelings, Lieutenant. However, I had a duty to my client," he bowed to Victoria, "and it is for her sake and her future happiness, that I felt obligated to reveal the truth."

Myers and Victoria snapped their heads towards Holmes when he said, 'her future happiness'. Then they looked sheepishly at each other. Westwood noticed but said nothing. At that juncture, Holmes and I chose to leave the young folk to work out their plans for informing the Colonel and we returned to the Falstaff Inn for lunch.

Two days later we were whisking our way by train back to London. The Colonel, though furious at first, was placated once he again saw his true son, and actually thanked Corporal Myers for being so loyal to his commanding officer.

After sufficient convalescence, Lieutenant Westwood returned home and was eventually able to obtain work doing architectural design. Myers was a frequent guest and after a suitable time, he and Victoria were married. He now has a bait and tackle shop at the harbour.

During the interval, when we received their wedding invitation, Holmes remarked, "I am happy for them Watson. This is a fortunate denouement. Revealing the whole truth could just as easily have had disastrous results."

"Holmes, you are far too cynical."

"Perhaps, Watson, but I have read somewhere that cynicism is a sign of genius."

"Well then, I'm glad you are the genius, instead of me."

I must confess that I did not appreciate the look he gave me after my remark.

Chapter Twelve

A Compromise

I sympathised with Holmes's plight. I knew that he sometimes held back the truth if he felt justified. But I also knew that he took his professional obligations to his clients seriously.

"You have not yet confronted Lieutenant Westwood, I presume?"

"I would not think of rushing into an emotionally charged situation without the benefit of your counsel, Doctor," he replied. "To confront the younger Westwood would be to invite flight, or perhaps even suicide, depending upon his commitment to keeping his secret.

"You are the better judge of the fair sex, Watson. I need your opinion of Miss Westwood. She seems a headstrong young woman and I am not sure that she would believe me if I told her I found no evidence of fraud."

I recalled a similar case involving Miss Mary Sutherland back in '88[1] but, based on her personality, he would not tell her all he knew. On that occasion Holmes only advised her that her fiancé was gone forever and that she should move on. I knew this would not work on Victoria Westwood and said as much.

"You have read her correctly, Holmes," I remarked. "She is intelligent, proud, headstrong, and too observant for Myers to

---

[1] *A Case of Identity* by Arthur Conan Doyle published in *The Strand Magazine* in September 1891.

be able to fool forever. I've no doubt that she would continue to pursue the matter even if you bow out with the conclusion that she was in error."

He thought for a few moments as he puffed away at his pipe, the smoke curling towards the open window as it caught the suction of a passing breeze. Finally, he pointed the stem at me and said, "Here's what I need you to arrange."

The following morning after 'Charles' had left on his morning drive, I advised the Colonel that I needed to check on my patient but would be home for lunch. As prearranged the evening before, Victoria announced that she was going to visit a friend and asked if I would escort her as it was not far and in the same direction I was going.

We again met 'Captain Basil' at the Falstaff Inn and stepped into the pub where we found a quiet corner, the breakfast crowd having departed. Once seated, she leaned forward, staring into Holmes's eyes and urged him to tell her what news he had.

Holmes looked sternly into her eyes and said, "I do have some news. I have solved your case, but you must prepare yourself for the outcome."

Her countenance fell and she whispered, "Is Charles dead then?"

Holmes shook his head and said, "No, but he is not well."

"You've seen him?" she asked, hopefully.

"He is at a convalescent centre in Dumpton. I've observed him from afar whilst he slept and I've seen his medical chart. His prognosis is not good. He, like the man who is impersonating him, has lost an eye, but he has also lost a leg, has severe damage to his throat and lungs, and can only speak in short, raspy tones."

"But will he live?" she pleaded.

As a medical man, I felt it prudent to reply, "His healing will depend much on his spirit and will to live. The fact that he has arranged this imposter to take his place does not speak well for his self-confidence."

"Who is this imposter that he would take my brother's place?"

Holmes answered, "A man from your brother's platoon. Lance Corporal William Myers. He was in the same action that nearly killed your brother, and received similar injuries but to the opposite side of his body."

She sat back and digested this flood of information. Then she straightened up and, with a determined set to her jaw, demanded, "I must see Charles! Will you take me to him?"

I spoke up again, "Your brother has gone to great lengths to keep his condition from you and your father. Are you sure you wish to expose his secret against his wishes?"

She responded firmly, "I believe the shock of his injuries has affected him. I will not let him die alone just so he can spare my feelings. Please, Mr. Holmes, take me to him now."

"If we go now," I said, "we may catch him and Myers together. Are you sure you want that?"

She looked at me and, after a split-second hesitation, said, "Yes, let's get it all out in the open.

We paid a cab driver extra to make haste to the Holy Trinity Convalescent Centre and upon arrival saw that the Benz Motorwagen was still parked in front. Holmes, led the way, explaining to a nurse who recognised him as the visiting doctor from before, that he was bringing family members to see a patient.

As we walked down the hallway towards the private room that Westwood had due to his critical condition, we encountered Corporal Myers just leaving. He froze at the sight of Victoria, gave a quick glance at me, then rushed towards us, "You can't be here! Victoria, trust me, you do not want to know what I'm doing here!"

He started to reach for her arm as if trying to guide her away but she slapped his hand aside. "I know what you're doing here, *Corporal Myers* and I will see my real brother!"

He turned his appeal to me, "Dr. Watson, if you know his secret you know why she should not go in. Please!"

"It is her wish and you should know how headstrong she is. You had best come with us."

We all went into the room. Lieutenant Westwood was lying on his side, attempting to read a Bible with his one eye. He looked up at the sound of the door opening and started at the number of people entering. Then he saw his sister.

"Vicky? My God! What are you doing here?"

She ran to his bedside but he turned away "No! Don't look at me! Remember the brother you once had. Not this wretched wreck which I have become. Please go away!"

But she would not leave his side. Though his back was now to her, she held his shoulders, leaned her head into his neck and cried, "It's all right, Chucky. I'm here and everything is going to be all right."

He turned back and took her by the shoulders, "No! It's *never* going to be all right unless you do as I say. You and Will go home and keep pretending he is me. Do *not* tell father about me. Promise me! He must never know what a decrepit creature his son has become. Will tells me that he has been able to fool him so far, even if he has not fooled you since you're here."

He let her go and looked down, "I knew you would be the hardest to deceive. Father was gone so much he hardly knew me, but the two of us growing up together …" He looked back up at her, and whispered in his raspy voice, "You stubborn little girl."

She crossed her arms and responded, "If loving one's own brother is stubborn, then I am guilty as charged. I know your secret now and I don't care. I want us to be together."

Westwood shook his head, "I may never leave this place. The shrapnel that penetrated my chest permanently damaged my left lung. There is still a piece in there that is too close to my heart for them to risk removing. A wrong move, a fall, or even a coughing fit could be fatal. If I am here doctors may be able to save me. I cannot go home. I will not put you in a position to witness my death, and Will here can be a suitable substitute for the son father barely knew."

"But …"

He held up his hand, "No 'buts'. The Corporal has his orders and has no other family to return to. I have been able to feed him information to maintain the deception. I've given him access to my bank funds so that he can pay my expenses. You must keep up this pretence for Father's sake, as well as my own. I beg you, Vicky."

Strong as she was, the emotional situation brought her to her knees at her brother's bedside and she cried into his shoulder. When her sobs subsided she looked upon him with reddened eyes and nodded. "But I will still come visit you as often as I can!" she insisted.

He patted her head and nodded, "Thank you, dear sister. Just one more question, who are these other gentlemen, and will they keep our secret?"

She pointed to me, "That is Dr. John Watson. He served with father at Maiwand and is staying with us for a few days. And that is his friend, the famous detective Sherlock Holmes. He is the one who discovered your deception."

Holmes stepped forward, "I am sorry for your situation, Lieutenant. I assure you that Dr. Watson and I will keep our silence, until such time comes as you, or your sister, release us from it."

With that Holmes and I left the young folk to talk out their issues. I ended my visit to the Colonel two days later, citing a need to return to London. On the train home, Holmes asked, "I presume all is going well in the Westwood household?"

"*Well* being a relative term," I replied. "The Colonel is none the wiser. Victoria and the Corporal are playing their brother-sister act nicely. However, I still see signs of a budding romance there and I do not know how they will handle that situation should their feelings become more than sibling affection."

Holmes nodded, then surprised me with this observation, "I believe it was Shakespeare who said that 'the course of true love never did run smooth'[1]. Perhaps the turbulence of their course will be proof their love is true when realised."

---

[1] *A Midsummer Night's Dream* Act 1 Scene 1, said by Lysander to Hermia.

Editor's Note: Less than a year after my visit, Colonel Westwood died from cancer. Will Myers and Victoria Westwood got married and moved to Broadstairs to be closer to her brother. Lieutenant Charles Westwood died in his sleep at the convalescent centre four months after his father's death.

Taurus: The Bull
(20th April – 20th May)

The Case of
John Bull vs. Britannia

Loyal to a fault, a Taurean is the most reliable person that you can have in your corner when the chips are down. However, they have a stubborn streak a mile wide and can hold a grudge like no one else, so make sure that you don't cross them.

Chapter One

It was June 1883, shortly after we had completed the adventure that I have recorded elsewhere as *How Green Was My Valet?*[1] It was mid-morning and Holmes was examining the daily newspapers in search of a possible new case. I was organising my notes on our latest adventure when the doorbell rang. The tread on the stairs indicated our landlady, Mrs. Hudson, was showing a guest up to our rooms. She knocked and, when invited to come in, she was accompanied by a rather astonishing sight.

"A gentleman to see you, Mr. Holmes," she announced in her pleasant Scottish accent, at which point the fellow behind her stepped up to her side. He was short and stout of late middle age by the looks of him. The remarkable aspect of him was his attire.

He wore a dark blue tailcoat, white breeches, black boots, a low topper hat and a waistcoat patterned as the Union flag. In other words, he was the spitting image[2] of John Bull[3], every political cartoonist's representation of Great Britain. He pointed at my companion and cried, "Sherlock Holmes, I need you!"

---

[1] *The Colourful Cases of Sherlock Holmes, Volume 4* by Roger Riccard and published by Baker Street Studios Limited in 2025.
[2] The concept and phrase were in circulation by 1689, when George Farquhar used it in his play *Love and a Bottle*: 'Poor child! He's as like his own dada as if he were spit out of his mouth'.
[3] Image of John Bull was used on World War I recruiting posters.

Holmes gazed up from behind *The Daily News* and said, "Yes, I imagine you do, Mr. Robert John Bullbank. Do sit down. Thank you, Mrs. Hudson."

Our visitor seemed a little taken aback at this pronouncement and entered the room slowly now, instead of at the energetic pace he had previously displayed. He removed his hat and sat in the chair indicated whilst Holmes folded his paper and set it aside.

"Where did you get my full name?" he asked. "I haven't used it in years."

Holmes replied, "It is my business to know things. In your case, I had a client in the past with a shop near yours, and during my investigation, I looked into the backgrounds of all the neighbouring establishments. That is how I discovered that, for business purposes, you shortened your real name to John Bull. "

Turning to me he said, "Watson please be good enough to offer Mr. Bull a cigar, for I see that he has forgotten his snuff box and he is a decidedly jumpy from a lack of nicotine."

I held out our cigar box to him and he gratefully took one of the *Piedras* and lit it. Then he asked, "How did you know that I had forgotten my snuff box, Mr. Holmes?"

Holmes waved his hand as if it were a foolish question but deigned to answer it all the same, "Your waistcoat is part of your daily costume therefore it has taken on, not only the shape of your physique but also become creased by the objects you habitually keep in your pockets. Your pocket watch is in your right-hand pocket as its circular shape has left its impression there. Therefore when I see the rectangular outline on your left pocket lying loose from emptiness, I conclude the missing snuff box. This arrangement also tells me that you are right-handed, as you take out your snuff box with your left hand and gather a pinch of the powder with your right.

"But that is of small consequence compared to the reason for your visit. What can you tell me of the substitution, that has not already appeared in the press?"

I was at a loss as to what Holmes was talking about until he held up the newspaper that he had been reading and I realised it was one of the morning editions that I had not read yet. From where I sat all I could make out was a picture of a statue of Britannia.

"Well, for one thing, I can tell you the police are baffled, which is why I've come to you."

Holmes smirked and then asked, "For the sake of Dr. Watson, who has not had a chance to read of your mishap, please tell us all that has occurred."

I pulled out a pencil and paper as Bull sat up straight and waved his cigar in our direction. "It was the night before last that it happened. Sometime between close of business Saturday, and Sunday morning when I was passing by my shop on the way to church. Someone stole the statue of John Bull that sits outside my shop and substituted a statue of Britannia. You can see the picture, there in the paper."

Holmes handed it to me but kept his eyes on our client, bidding him to continue.

"My statue, rather the *John Bull* statue as the face does not resemble me, is carved from solid mahogany and has a weighted base to keep it from being knocked over. Altogether it weighs about 15 stone.

"This new statue is so bulky that three constables could not budge it. It appears to be made of bronze with a heavy wooden base."

Holmes asked, "Is it larger than your John Bull statue?"

"Oh, yes, Mr. Holmes, not so much the statue itself, but the base it sits on is quite a bit bigger. It nearly takes up the whole pavement between my shop front and the street."

"Is it in the same spot as your old statue?"

"Well, as I said, Mr. Holmes, the base is bigger, but yes, it completely covers the spot where my statue stood."

"And you've received no note of explanation. No ransom demand for your old statue or anything of the sort?"

"Not a word, Mr. Holmes."

"Have you noticed anyone paying particular attention to it lately or taking measurements?"

"No, no one like that."

"As I recall, yours is a curio shop, selling novelties, antiques and the like, especially patriotic items. Have any of your customers complained lately?"

Bull puffed himself up with pride, "I only sell quality items, not cheap junk like some others. No one has ever complained about my merchandise."

Holmes sat back and tapped his pipe stem to his lips. Finally, he said, "I shall be happy to look into the matter for you. Who is the inspector on the case?"

Chapter Two

Holmes was pleased to hear that Inspector Lestrade was assigned to the investigation. He immediately suggested that we return to our client's shop, *The Bullpen*, and examine the crime scene. Afterwards, we would continue on to Scotland Yard to consult with the Inspector.

During our cab ride, Holmes assured our client, "Lestrade is one of Scotland Yard's best men, Mr. Bull. We have worked with him before. He is tenacious as a bulldog and won't quit until he gets his man. I am sure that, between the Doctor, myself and him, we shall have your statue back in place quickly."

He then turned away from our client and gave me a small smirk and a wink. Lestrade was tenacious, as my companion had said, but he was also lacking in imagination and often found himself at sixes and sevens in the middle of a case, which was usually when he called on Holmes for assistance.

We arrived at Bull's shop on Notting Hill Gate just west of Kensington Gardens, where passersby were admiring the Britannia statue. It was really a beautiful monument and the bronze reflected the brilliant sunlight on this bright summer's day. Whoever the artist was, they showed a clear talent for bronze work. I wondered if that fact would be useful in Holmes's investigation.

The wooden base seemed to be walnut with a beautiful grain pattern, which complemented the bronze of the sculpture. Holmes took several measurements and examined the base closely with his magnifying lens. Stepping up on the base, he also made close scrutiny of the bronze work. He knocked on the metal in several places and made notes. Then he stepped down and turned his gaze towards the street looking up and down. I could not tell what he was searching for and asked, "Are you thinking the artist is nearby, admiring his work, Holmes?"

He smiled at something or someone he saw, but I could not discern who, as a small group of pedestrians were walking away on the other side of the street. "Possibly, Watson. But I was primarily admiring the location the artist chose."

I looked around. There were several shops up and down the street. None of them stood out to me in any peculiar way, and I said as much to Holmes. The detective replied, "You are putting limitations on yourself, Doctor. Expand your vision and let your imagination see why Britannia is appropriate to this particular location."

I frowned and he shook his head, "Well think on it, Watson, while we take a ride to visit friend Lestrade at the Yard."

Inspector Lestrade was a gentleman I remembered from my early days living with Holmes at Baker Street before I knew his occupation. The weasel-faced fellow was a frequent visitor seeking advice. I got to know him better during the case that I would later publish as *A Study in Scarlet*[1]. His office at Scotland Yard seemed to be an organisation of piles of paper. It was not quite as untidy as my companion kept our study, but it was far from prim and proper.

We found the fellow seated at his desk reading through a file. When he looked up and saw us, he frowned. "Hello, Mr. Holmes, Doctor Watson. No offence, but I hope that you are not here to bring me some new crime. As you can see, I am quite busy."

"On the contrary, Lestrade!" Holmes boomed out with enthusiasm. "We are here to assist on the John Bull case."

---

[1] By Arthur Conan Doyle and first published in *Beeton's Christmas Annual* in 1887.

"Ah, well that's different. You're more than welcome to give me any information or advice on that one. Seems like a silly prank to me, but a theft is a theft."

"May I enquire as to what steps you have taken?" asked Holmes.

"We've narrowed down the time of the incident due to the timetable of the constable beats in that neighbourhood and determined that it occurred between three-thirty and four in the morning. I am also looking into haulage companies with crane equipment. As I see it, the culprits must have arrived in two vehicles. One, a large wagon with the Britannia statue. The other, a portable crane wagon to lift away the John Bull statue and replace it with Britannia. Then they drove away with the John Bull."

Holmes cocked his head, blinked an eye and replied, "You believe that they drove into position, moved the John Bull statue aside, then changed the harness to the Britannia statue and placed it precisely in the position where John Bull was, then moved the harness again to the John Bull statue so they could raise it onto the empty space on the wagon vacated by the Britannia statue, then drove off, all in the space of thirty minutes?"

The Inspector shook his head, "I know that it sounds difficult, Mr. Holmes, and it must have taken a very efficient crew. But I can think of no other explanation."

Holmes shook his head and mumbled, "No." Louder he stated, "This portable crane wagon must be extremely rare."

Lestrade admitted, "Well, I've never actually seen one, Mr. Holmes, but what other explanation is there?"

The detective looked at me, then up at the ceiling, as if trying to make a decision. Finally. he informed Lestrade of his deductions.

The Inspector gazed upon him in astonishment, "Are you sure, Mr. Holmes?"

"It's elementary, Inspector. Any other explanation is much too cumbersome."

"You've solved it then?"

"Only half of it," answered my friend. "We know how the statues were exchanged, but we need to find out by who and why."

Chapter Three

I spoke up, "How do we do that, Holmes? Why would anyone wish to substitute Britannia for John Bull?"

"That is the question," replied the detective. "When we answer *why* then we will be dull indeed if we cannot determine *who*."

He paused, then turned to the Inspector, "Lestrade, I suggest that you look for a moving van large enough to transport the Britannia sculpture. Keep me informed of your progress. I shall be at Baker Street."

Off we went to our home. Holmes was silent during the cab ride and I did not interrupt him. But once back in our sitting room, I questioned his purpose for returning here.

"I need to think, Watson," he replied. "This is at least a two, possibly three-pipe problem. I also need to be around my reference books and newspapers should an idea present itself. I beg you not to speak to me for at least the next hour. In fact, why don't you step out and purchase the afternoon papers?"

He reached for the Persian slipper hung on the mantel and filled it with tobacco as he pulled out his old briar pipe. As he did so I stepped out of the door, satisfied in knowing that Holmes had determined where the John Bull statue was even if we didn't know why it was switched.

I took some time gathering up the afternoon editions. I decided to stop at a nearby pub for a glass of ale before returning to the aura of cognitive manipulation which I knew would permeate the atmosphere of our rooms, not to mention the choking clouds of smoke from Holmes's pipe.

Imagine my surprise then, to find the room free of tobacco smoke, and Holmes missing from his favourite chair. I called down to our landlady, "Mrs. Hudson?"

She stepped out of her kitchen to the bottom of our staircase, "Oh, Dr. Watson, you're back. I am sorry I did not hear you come in. Mr. Holmes said to tell you that 'the game is afoot' and then he left in his vicar disguise and said that he would not be home until dinner. You are to skim the newspapers for anything related to women's groups."

I thoughtfully tilted my head and replied, "Thank you, Mrs. Hudson. Could I have a pot of tea please?"

She nodded and returned to the kitchen while I sat in my usual chair, lit a cigar, and settled in with the afternoon editions. The only relevant item I noted was a small notice of a meeting of S.O.W.E.R., the Society Of Women's Equal Rights. It was to be held the following afternoon at Burnfield Hall on Holland Park Avenue near Norland Square.

Most historical women's clubs served social and charitable purposes. These have included voluntary civic service purposes such as: opening lending libraries and seeking funding to create permanent public libraries, pursuing historic preservation, advocating for women's suffrage (and other rights for women), serving as professional women's clubs (comparable to historic men's clubs of London), serving as athletic clubs or otherwise supporting sports and physical activity, addressing sanitation and health issues, hosting social activities (including card games), hosting lectures and otherwise engaging in education, and addressing employment and labour conditions

The passage of the Married Women's Property Act of 1882, which became effective on 1st January 1883, resulted in a flurry of such groups arising to keep pushing the women's movement for equal rights forward. I set the notice aside for Holmes's review upon his return.

I found no other stories or notices of the type Holmes had me seeking, but did find a few articles of interest to me. These kept me occupied the rest of the afternoon and well into the evening. Holmes returned just after seven-thirty when the sun was low in the summer sky. I had only just turned up the lamps in the sitting room when he strode in, removed his moustache, spectacles, clerical collar and priest's hat, poured himself a whisky and dropped into his chair with an air of satisfaction.

"You must have had an epiphany shortly after I left you, Holmes," I stated. "Was this particular disguise essential, or did you merely assume the easiest at hand?"

"Ah, Watson, there are times when I even surprise myself," he replied. "I seem to have developed an instinct which takes over my mind without a second thought. If you had asked me what disguise would have worked for the task today I could have given you a list of half a dozen. But choosing this particular one hid my features and allowed me access to our suspect as a trusted soul."

"You have a suspect?"

"Indeed."

I handed him the S.O.W.E.R. meeting notice and asked, "Do they have anything to do with these people?"

My companion read the notice and chuckled, "Watson, you have hit upon the very group wherein my focus lies."

"How did you discover them?" I asked.

"You asked me this morning as I was gazing across the street, if I was seeking out the perpetrator of our crime. As I recall, I advised you that I had determined a possible reason for the location chosen, in addition to searching the crowd for an admiring foe. Have you thought any more along those lines, my friend?"

I shook my head as I was not sure my answer would meet his satisfaction, "All I could come up with was that John Bull's shop is known for its patriotic goods and that someone seeking publicity for their artistry in creating the Britannia bronze would wish to appeal to that type of crowd."

To my surprise, he applauded, "Excellent, Watson! You have indeed hit upon a very important aspect of the crime. If we can indeed call it such. The other side of that coin is the substitution of a female representation of Great Britain for a male depiction."

I had stood and was pouring myself a brandy as a precursor to dinner, when I replied, "Hence your interest in the S.O.W.E.R. group. You believe that they intend to take advantage of this substitution to publicise their cause."

"Not just take advantage, Doctor," responded Holmes. "They are the ones who perpetrated the act precisely so they could call attention to themselves and their cause."

"So what will you do now?"

"I have sent an invitation for ten o'clock tomorrow morning to the head of S.O.W.E.R., Mrs. Evangeline Hammersmith, and her husband. I have also asked Mr. Bull to drop by at ten thirty. If all goes well, I suspect we can relieve Inspector Lestrade of any further police involvement in this case.

Chapter Four

At precisely ten o'clock the following morning, Mrs. Hudson showed up a remarkable couple. Mr. Albert Hammersmith was a barrel-chested fellow, nearly as tall as Holmes but weighing considerably more at about sixteen stone. I guessed his age to be in his early thirties as his hair was a thick, rich chestnut brown with a moustache to match. His wife was equally exceptional in that she was broad-shouldered and tall, perhaps five foot nine as her amber eyes were barely lower than mine when we exchanged greetings. Her hair was light brown, long and straight as it hung down her back nearly to her waist. The hand that shook mine was large and strong and the nails were short. I would have put her slightly younger than her husband. Perhaps twenty-eight or so.

They declined refreshment as the husband got straight to business, "What was the meaning of your invitation, Mr. Holmes? Who are you and what do you think you know?"

Holmes stood while I sat and took notes, "In the interest of time let me answer your questions and tell you what I know without interruption, for Mr. John Bull will be arriving at ten-thirty."

The couple looked at each other, unable to hide their surprise or fear at this revelation. Holmes took a beat to let them digest that statement, then commenced his narrative.

"I am a private detective, hired by Mr. Bull. First I will tell you what I know, then I will give you my speculations and you may confirm or deny them. I know that in the early morning hours of Sunday last, you, Mr. Hammersmith, backed your moving van up to the front of John Bull's shop and, using the boom and pulley system inside, lowered the hollow, bronze Britannia statue over top of the John Bull statue. You then bolted the nameplate onto the Britannia statue using long enough woodscrews to attach it to the base of the John Bull statue so that it would appear heavier than it actually is."

Before the husband could interrupt, Holmes turned to the lady, "You, Mrs. Hammersmith, are the sculptor of that fine bronze piece. Your hands betray your work with the plaster castings and your hair retains the indentations where you frequently tie it back to keep it out of your way.

"You chose John Bull's shop for three reasons. One, which my colleague, Dr. Watson discerned, was that you wished to draw publicity to your work among patrons who favoured patriotic works. Two, you wished to call attention to the fact that women can represent Great Britain as well as men, and thus should have equal rights. Finally, his shop lies on the road to Kensington Palace, where many royal family members and politicians are likely to behold it."

Holmes paused to enquire, "Are you sure that you will not take some refreshment? Mrs. Hudson's tea is excellent." They each shook their heads and the detective continued his narrative.

"I met with each of you yesterday, where you inadvertently took me into your confidence. As the Reverend Homer Cousins, I came to you, Mrs. Hammersmith, at Burnfield Hall, where I had followed you, after seeing you admiring your work from across the street from John Bull's shop. As you recall, I watched you rehearsing the speech that you are planning to give today. Your intentions were clear in that you believed your group should use Britannia as their symbol of strong women. Comparing her with America's Columbia, France's Marianne, Lady Justice and Queens Elizabeth and Victoria was quite inspiring. When you finished, I questioned you about your stance versus the traditional Bible roles so often quoted by the clergy. Again, you eloquently reminded me of the stories of Ruth, Deborah, Esther and Mary as well as the proverb of the smart businesswoman who inspects a field, buys it and makes it profitable. All during that discussion I was observing your hands, hair and other physical characteristics that identified you as a sculptor."

Turning to her husband, Holmes continued, "As to you, sir, no doubt you recall my coming by your business after learning of your trade from your wife, who likes to promote your agreement to her beliefs despite being in a manly trade such as moving and storage. I asked you about transporting a statue we had ordered from Italy from the docks to our parish and you showed me your moving van with the boom and pulley system which would ensure safe transport and delivery."

Holmes stopped to let them digest what he had revealed. Finally, the husband asked, "What now, Mr. Holmes? Are you going to the police?"

Holmes rubbed his hands together and replied, "Mr. Bull will be here soon. If you wish, you may leave and I will merely tell him that his statue is still in place underneath Britannia and all he has to do is unbolt the nameplate and hire someone, perhaps the Hammersmith Removals and Storage Company, to lift it off and haul it away. With his statue back in prominence, the perpetrator will not really be that important to him and I believe that he will not pursue the matter. He may even decide to leave the Britannia statue outside the front of his shop as well. One on either side of his door should make a nice display and certainly, the perpetrator will not seek its return for fear of being charged.

"On the other hand," continued the detective. "We may all meet with him together and explain your motives. I believe that we can convince him to not only refuse charges but to embrace the Britannia as a fixture for his business. While I was observing you from inside his shop yesterday, Mrs. Hammersmith, I noticed that he has a great many female clientele purchasing decorations, toys and gifts. If he can be convinced of the benefits of supporting at least some aspects of your movement, it would work out well for all concerned. I also believe, should you wish it so, that I can keep both your names a secret."

The lady spoke up, "How will you explain our presence here then?"

"If you will trust me I can explain that easily enough in a way that, should he be disagreeable, will allow you to leave with him none the wiser."

The husband and wife discussed it briefly and decided to take Holmes up on his offer. They also took tea while we awaited the arrival of John Bull.

The shop owner arrived exactly on time and began to question Holmes before he noticed that there were others in the room. "Have you found it, Mr. Holmes? I ... oh, I beg your pardon. I did not realise that you had visitors."

Holmes responded in his smoothest and most affable manner, "Quite all right, Mr. Bull. Allow me to introduce Mr. and Mrs. Hammersmith. They have offered to assist with your case."

"Assist? How?" asked the shopkeeper as he removed his hat, bowed to our guests and sat down.

"First, let me explain that your John Bull statue is not missing at all. The Britannia statue is hollow and was lowered over it, then fastened to it by the bolts in the nameplate so it could not be moved."

"What!? It's been there the whole time?" sputtered the shopkeeper.

"It was really the only logical explanation," replied Holmes smoothly. "Switching the statues for each other would have been far too cumbersome and time-consuming."

Bull nodded his assent and asked, "But then, how can these people help?"

Holmes in his most persuasive tone said, "They have offered to assist with the removal of Britannia. Mr. Hammersmith owns a removals and storage company and can safely lift off Britannia without damaging your John Bull statue underneath. Mrs. Hammersmith is the head of a women's organisation that would like to use the Britannia bronze as a symbol of their movement.

Bull nodded, "That would be fine with me, as long as I get my statue back. It is the symbol of my store after all."

At a signal from Holmes, I handed Bull a cup of tea. In addition to providing a relaxed atmosphere, it would also prod him to stay for Holmes's next proposition. "We were all just discussing that very thing," said Holmes. "I noticed that in your shop yesterday, the majority of the customers were women."

"That's true enough," replied the merchant.

Holmes continued, "Mrs. Hammersmith suggested that perhaps you would wish to keep the Britannia statue and have each of them flanking your front door, to attract buyers of both genders. In return, she would be happy to promote your shop among members of her society. All she would ask is that they could occasionally have a photograph taken for publicity purposes. Publicity, that would also reflect favourably upon your shop."

The living image of England sipped his tea, then set down the cup and said, "Mrs. Bull would certainly be in favour of that. She's always off marching for this and that cause for women's rights. I have to admit I was in favour of the Married Women's Property Act. If anything happened to me I would certainly want my Abigail to inherit it all rather than that no-good brother of mine."

He took another moment and finally replied, "All right, on one condition."

"Yes?" replied Evangeline Hammersmith.

"You can publicise any cause you like with those photographs as long as they do not show the name of my shop in anything that promotes women's suffrage. I'll not have my name connected with supporting votes for women."

Holmes and I turned to the lady in apprehension. I saw her stiffen and her fingers curled into fists, but her husband gently laid a hand upon her forearm and said, "Considering all the other women's causes there are, that seems reasonable. Doesn't it my dear?"

I could see his fingers tighten ever so slightly as he endeavoured to calm his wife. She took a breath, and forced a smile, "I believe that would be acceptable, Mr. Bull."

I saw her mouth form another syllable but no more sound came forth.

"Well then," he slapped his hands upon his knees and stood. "When can you lift Britannia and arrange the statues, Mr. Hammersmith?"

"I'll have a crew come by at noon tomorrow," answered the removal man.

"Well, fine." Then turning to my friend he said, "If you find out who did this, Holmes, you can just tell him I'm keeping the statue and he can't have it back. That'll teach him for disturbing private property."

"I will do that, Mr. Bull," answered Holmes. "I will also inform Inspector Lestrade that you will not be pressing charges and that he can cease his investigation."

"Fine, fine," waved the stout merchant who then bowed to our guests, put his hat back upon his head and strode out of the door as if he were England off to inspect the Empire.

Once he was safely out of earshot, Mrs. Hammersmith started to spew a host of invectives directed at our client. Her husband, however, let out a sigh of relief. "Thank you, Mr. Holmes."

My friend, ever the diplomatist, turned his attention upon the lady, "Mrs. Hammersmith let me point out one prominent fact that you are forgetting."

"What's that?" she seethed.

"Bull said the name of his shop could not be in any photos used to promote women's suffrage. I do believe that your husband could place the statue of Britannia in such a way that you will be able to gather members of your group around it and have an angle that will not include the name of the shop in the background."

"Yes, I think I know just how to place it. Problem solved! You get everything you wished for, darling!"

With that realisation, Evangeline lifted her teacup to my flatmate, smiled and said, "Thank you, Mr. Holmes. And you can tell *Reverend Cousins* that he is welcome to our meetings anytime.

After the couple had left us, I turned to the detective and said, "You have made your opinion of women quite clear in the past, Holmes. What made you take the lady's side in this matter?"

Holmes sat down and lit his churchwarden pipe. Pointing the long stem at me he replied, "I have come to realise that denying benefits to deserving women because of the actions of some foolish females is not just, Doctor. The more I see of mankind, the more I am aware that there are also men who are worthless to actually cast an intelligent vote, or receive rights and privileges denied to the fair sex, simply because of their gender. In my discussion with Mrs. Hammersmith yesterday as Reverend Cousins, I found her arguments compelling. Thus, at least for this instance, I have chosen to amend my former opinion. But, Watson ..."

"Yes, Holmes?"

"Do not hold me to it in every case."

Gemini: The Twins
(21st May – 20th April)

The Gemini Pearl Necklace

Gemini is accordingly excellent at guiding change and transformation. These curious people are terrific pioneers, using their energy to spearhead innovative creative projects. A fearless thinker, Gemini is always down to try something new or design something unique.

Chapter One

The winter of 1898 found me accompanying my friend, the detective, Sherlock Holmes, to spend Christmas in Aylesbury with his old college history teacher, Professor Christopher Nichols. I had met the Professor the first time we visited his dairy farm during the Yuletide of 1882. That was the time when Holmes had helped the newly retired academic discover the orphan his cook had taken in was, in reality, his ten-year-old daughter.[1]

It was she, the former Tina Monroe, who invited us to come and spend a festive break. She was married now to the business manager of the farm, Noel Everest, and had a four-year-old daughter of her own, named Marjorie, after her mother. They pretty much ran the estate now, the Professor being in his early seventies and in failing health.

We arrived just before noon on Thursday 22nd December, under high clouds and cool temperatures. The driver from Nichols's farm greeted us warmly, "Mr. Holmes, Dr. Watson, it is good of you to come. Mrs. Everest hopes that your presence will help restore the Professor's memories to some extent. He used to speak of your last visit with affection and still marvels at your marksmanship with his Colt .45s."

---

[1] Details can be found in *The Eighth Milkmaid*, in *Sherlock Holmes: Adventures for The Twelve Days of Christmas* published by Baker Street Studios Limited in 2015.

"His memories are fading then?" I asked with concern, as he loaded our luggage.

"I am afraid so, Doctor. He can remember things from many years ago, but recent events have become difficult for him to recall."

He opened the carriage door, pointing out the traveling rugs, and said, "You'll see for yourselves, gentlemen. He has good days and bad days. The mistress hopes that your presence will give him one more good Christmas to remember. Go ahead and wrap up. I'll have you out to the farm in a moment."

True to his word, the drive passed quickly. Coming upon our first sight of the farm it was much as I remembered it. The same structures, paddocks, and pastureland. A light snow from a previous storm had left white patches scattered about. Coming upon the main house, the outside was festooned with holly boughs and a large wreath. One welcome addition since our last visit was a large portico which now extended out over the drive allowing us to disembark under its shelter as we entered the house. Servants came out to pick up our luggage and as I looked towards the open front door, I saw a beautiful young lady in her mid-twenties. I tapped Holmes on the elbow as he was looking out upon the grounds, pointed in the direction of the lady, and said, "That must be Tina. My, she has grown into a beauty!"

Holmes turned and, for one of the few times in my association with him, froze. I noted his stare at the woman and after several seconds I chose to break the impasse before it became rude. "Holmes, shall we go and re-introduce ourselves?"

With a quick shake of his head, he took a deep breath, looked at me, and whispered, "Sorry, Doctor. I was not prepared. She is the living image of her mother "

I recalled Holmes had been socially involved with Marjorie Monroe during his college years, but she had become impregnated with her daughter when she voluntarily took to caring for Professor Nichols when he was suffering deliriums upon the death of his wife. In her admiration for the man, she had allowed herself to succumb to her own feelings when he reached for her upon calling out his wife's name during one of his delirious episodes. That action, which he had no recollection of when he recovered, had resulted in her pregnancy and leaving town. Holmes, at that age, was bitterly disappointed at her unexplained disappearance. It was not until we visited Nichols sixteen years ago when Tina, newly orphaned, had arrived at the farm with her mother's diary, that he finally learned the truth.

Seeing his reaction now, set my imagination at work. Could it be Holmes's Bohemian lifestyle and his utter disregard for romantic involvement that was the result of that long ago relationship? Had his feelings for Marjorie Monroe been so deep that her disappearance forever carried away his capacity for emotional attachment? Was his distrust of the fair sex the consequence of his feelings of desertion at such an impressionable point in his life?

All these thoughts flashed through my mind as I started walking towards the entrance, giving his sleeve a slight tug. Still, we approached with smiles upon our faces and grace in our manner. She took my hand and I recalled the long fingers she had displayed as a child when she played the violin for us on that long ago Christmas. I bowed to her, "Mrs. Everest, thank you for your invitation."

"Oh, Doctor, surely you can call me Tina since you've known me from childhood." She then turned to my companion, "And you, sir, if I may be so bold, Papa has told me of how you cared for my mother during your university days and suggested that I should refer to you as uncle Sherlock. Do you mind?"

Holmes took a deep breath, kissed her outstretched hand, and replied, with as much emotion as I have ever seen in him, "As the odds of my ever having a niece in my bloodline are practically nil, I would be honoured for you to use such an appellation, Tina."

Greetings completed, Tina hooked her arm around Holmes's elbow and led us into the house where servants took our hats and coats. "Let me introduce you to my husband, then we'll go and see Papa."

Noel Everest was seated at the desk where we had first seen Professor Nichols working on a presentation the last time we were here. Though retired, his expertise in history at that time was still sought by several universities as a guest lecturer. Everest rose at our arrival and came out from behind the desk to greet us warmly.

"Mr. Holmes, Dr. Watson! Welcome to you both, gentlemen. Thank you for setting aside your plans to join us. I do hope your presence will encourage some improvement in the Professor's health."

Holmes shook the man's hand. He was perhaps two inches short of six feet with blond hair and blue eyes which spoke of a Nordic ancestry. I would put him a little older than Tina. Perhaps thirty or thereabouts, with a lean sinewy build. As I shook his hand, I noted my companion turn his gaze upon the desk. It was a force of habit for him, as intrusive as it was, especially since we were not on a case. Tina, of course, noted what her husband had not. "Is there something you need to know, uncle?"

Holmes shook his head, "I am sorry, my dear. My profession often overrides my manners. Forgive me. May we see the Professor?"

She turned towards the clock against the wall and said, "I will check on him. He often naps after lunch, but he may still be awake. Follow me."

We found the Professor in a sunroom in a corner of the west wing of the house. From there one could look out upon the pastures and see the livestock through large glass French doors which opened out upon a small patio. A fire was burning brightly in a hearth on the north wall, keeping the room well-heated. Nichols sat before it, his chair at a right angle so he could view the outdoors to the west. A luncheon tray was on a small table next to him and he was just setting down a glass of red wine.

In appearance, he certainly looked more frail than the gentleman I remembered. He had lost weight and his face was thinner, now more oval than round. His hair had stopped its recession and remained a short, white fringe around his bald head. His beard and moustache had grown thicker and longer. Had he not become so thin, he might have resembled Father Christmas taking a break from his workshop. As he turned to reach for his pipe, he caught sight of us out of the corner of his eye and turned to face us.

"Hello, Tina, my dear," he said cheerily. "Who have you brought to see me today, more teachers seeking my expertise?"

We strode forwards as a group with Tina in the lead, "I have a surprise for you Papa. This is your former student, Sherlock Holmes, and his friend Dr. Watson. Do you remember the last time they were here? It was the Christmas you adopted me."

Nichols adjusted the bifocals upon his nose as he gazed up at us. Then, with a great smile of recognition, pushed himself up from his seat and shuffled towards us. Holmes put out his hand, but the gentleman ignored it and threw his arms around my companion.

"Sherlock, my dear boy! How nice of you to come and see me!"

Holmes, unaccustomed to such displays of affection, especially from gentlemen, reacted a little stiffly, but then warmed to the embrace and patted his old Professor's back. When they parted, Nichols looked him up and down. "Still lean as an athlete and lithe as a cat."

Turning to me he cocked his head to one side as he put out his hand and said, "I know you, sir. *Doctor* Watson, you say? But that's not it. Medicine is not what comes to mind when I look upon you. I see you more as a formidable opponent. Did we ever debate with one another?"

I smiled as I shook the affable fellow's hand and replied, "I could hardly qualify to debate with you upon history, sir. But we did compete against each other last time I was here. It was in your cellar shooting gallery."

"Watson the pistoleer!" he cried with glee. "Welcome! Welcome! I hope you brought that Colt .45 I gave you. I should enjoy a rematch."

I smiled, bowed my head, and answered, "I should be happy to oblige, sir."

We all exchanged a few more pleasantries until Tina broke in with a suggestion, "Papa, uncle Sherlock, and Dr. Watson have not yet settled into their rooms. Perhaps we should let them do so while you take your afternoon nap. Then, in an hour or two, you can resume reminiscing."

The old man sighed in resignation. Looking in our direction, he offered, "See what I must put up with, gentlemen? A doting daughter always looking out for my best interests whether I wish it or not. I should like to continue this conversation, but I am afraid she's right. My afternoon naps have become so habitual I start yawning even before I've finished my lunch. You two go and get settled in and we'll get together later."

He paused, then added with great sincerity, "And thank you for coming. It will be a splendid Christmas with a full house."

We repaired to our rooms on the first floor. As I looked out upon the view from my window, noting the serene countryside and the holiday feeling in the air from the decorations scattered throughout the house, I thought to myself, what a pleasant way to spend Christmas, away from the hustle and bustle and crime of London. A relaxing break for both of us.

I should have known better ...

Chapter Two

I should explain to my readers, that not all of the trips Holmes and I embarked on for rest and recreation ended in a case. There were certainly times when the only deductions needed were where to find the best spot to catch fish. However, when one has a mind such as Holmes's and the habit of observing every little thing, it becomes inevitable he will discover puzzles or mysteries that are beyond the ken of most mortals and lead us into some sort of adventure to solve them. This was about to turn into one of those.

With bags unpacked and a change out of my traveling clothes, I returned downstairs. Before I saw any family members, I caught the scent of something baking and followed my nose to the kitchen. There I found Holmes, seated at a table and being poured a steaming cup of liquid by the cook. I was happy to see Mrs. Ricciardo again. Her hair was completely grey, as she herself would be in her late fifties by now. Seeing me she called out in that Italian-tinged accent of hers, "Dr. Watson, a pleasure to have you join us. *Venire, sedere,* please, come, sit and I pour you a nice hot mug of *cioccolato.*"

I did so and returned her compliment, "It's a pleasure to be here. I am glad to see you are still with the Professor, Mrs. Ricciardo. I still remember those delicious meals you prepared for us all those years ago."

"*Grazie, dottore,*" she said with a nod of modesty. "I can promise you are in for a feast on Christmas!"

I smiled and took a sip of the hot chocolate. It was Italian style, rich and thick, "Aah, *deliziosa, signora!*" I said, in my rudimentary Italian.

She giggled and returned to her stove. Turning to Holmes I asked, "What shall we do while we wait for the Professor, Holmes?"

His gaze turned towards the window where we could see high grey clouds with scattered patches of blue, "I was thinking of taking a turn about the grounds while the weather is holding. Storms could arrive any day and confine us to the house. I believe this would be an opportune time to take in the fresh country air."

"Excellent idea, Holmes," I agreed. Thus, upon finishing our drinks, we took up our ulsters and scarves and set off into the cool crisp afternoon. We strode westward towards the stream which separated the pastures from the woods. It was completely frozen over this time and the snow on the opposite bank in the shade of the woods was still a few inches thick.

Noting the slick grey surface of the twenty-foot-wide waterway, I remarked, "It appears there will be no fishing this trip. That ice looks quite thick."

"Thick enough for a man to walk upon," he replied.

"How can you tell that?" I asked.

He pointed a short distance away and said, "Because someone has!"

I looked in the direction he held his cane. I could see some disturbance in the snow along both banks and leading into the pasture. I followed in Holmes's footsteps as he approached the scene to get a closer look. Gazing down, I could see that there were holes in the mud and snow coming up the shallow slope of the bank. The actual tracks were indistinct, however. There was some curvature at each end, as you would expect of a heel or toe. Yet they were too wide and did not leave the natural shape of a boot, merely an oblong impression.

"These are the most unusual tracks I have ever seen," I remarked to my companion. "They are too deep for a snowshoe, but what kind of boot leaves a shape like that?"

Holmes had crouched and measured the length of the print and the stride. Straightening up he replied, "One worn by a person with nefarious purposes in mind."

I looked upon him quizzically and asked, "How can you tell he is nefarious by his footprints?"

He pointed to them and answered, "Because their shape is due to someone retracing their steps to distort the tracks. No friendly visitor would take such precautions. Let us see how far we can follow them."

Carefully we paralleled the path this strange visitor took. I should explain, that the pastures were not completely flat or level. Each had some slope to it, mostly towards the buildings, and the particular one we were in had some few mounds of boulders strewn about. Had the field been meant for crops, I'm sure these would have been cleared. As pastureland, however, there was no need. We followed the tracks to a spot where a person could crouch behind one of these boulder piles and have an excellent view of the barns, paddocks, and house.

"See how much the ground is disturbed here, Watson?" Holmes said, pointing with his stick. "The person who encroached upon this land stayed here for quite some time. Occasionally he would move around a bit, no doubt to keep from stiffening up during the cool of the evening."

"What leads you to conclude evening, Holmes? Could it not just as easily have been early morning?"

"Note the edges of the tracks, Watson. See how the mud has hardened? These tracks were made whilst the ground was still soft, then hardened with the freezing temperatures of the night. There has been some thawing today, but you can still see the minute cracks caused by the expansion of the soil as the water within froze and pushed upwards."

I pondered that, then suggested, "So someone, coming from the woods, hid behind these rocks in order to spy on the house. Do you suppose it was a burglar, casing the premises to learn the ways of the family, and when might be the opportune time to strike?"

Holmes leaned against the rocks and looked upon the dwellings below, "We lack data, Watson. Depending upon what the person was looking for, the target could be either the house or barn. We also do not know if he is a thief, or even if it is a man or woman for that matter. You remarked upon Tina's beauty. This person could be an admirer. They may be a kidnapper after the child, or an arsonist planning a fire. All we know at this point is that they appear to not wish their presence known."

Holmes attempted to backtrack the intruder's footsteps. We returned to the stream, crossed it, one at a time to be safe, and picked up the tracks on the wooded side. Unfortunately, we were unable to follow them very far. The rising and falling temperatures had caused melting snow to drop from the closely spaced trees and obliterate the tracks.

We continued our circumnavigation of the property. No other trespass signs presented themselves and we returned to the house, where Mrs. Ricciardo welcomed us each with a hot toddy. We took our drinks with us and made for the sitting room, doffing our outerwear to a servant along the way.

Chapter Three

In the sitting room, we found a roaring fire. Tina was knitting in a chair and upon the floor to one side of the hearth stood a large doll's house. Playing with figures of an appropriate scale, the child, Marjorie, sat on the rug in front of it. Unlike Tina, she did not take after her mother at all. A mass of blonde curls covered her head and hung in ringlets down the sides of her face. She wore a simple blue dress with white trim and stockings and when she turned towards the sound of our entrance, her face bore a strong resemblance to her father.

Tina introduced us saying, "Margie, this is your great-uncle Sherlock and his friend, Dr. Watson. They are friends of your grandfather and have come to share Christmas with us."

The little girl stood, walked over to us, and curtsied most properly, "I'm very pleased to meet you, gentlemen. Would you like to meet my dolls?" She reached out and took my hand, my being the closest to her, and led the way to the doll's house. It was quite a fanciful construct, with wings that opened up to reveal its many rooms. It was about three feet tall and just as wide. She picked up each figurine and held it up for Holmes and me to see. There was a man, a woman, a boy, a girl, a dog, and a cat, all with quite proper and fanciful names. Holmes and I congratulated her on her little doll family and moved to the sofa to delight in the warmth of the fire and our drinks.

"Did you enjoy your walk?" asked Tina, the consummate hostess wishing to see to all our comforts.

"It was quite refreshing," I answered, speaking first in my desire to assure her of our pleasure before Holmes went into his inevitable questions.

It was well I did so, for his reply to her was a request to speak with her and her husband alone if she would allow me to watch over the child. I nodded my assent, of course, and she, tilting her head with curiosity, agreed and stood, instructing Marjorie to keep me company. She then led Holmes off to meet with Noel.

He later related their conversation to me:

Entering the study, Noel was still at work on a ledger. He started to rise when his wife walked in with the detective, but Holmes waved him back into his seat as he closed the door behind him. Seating themselves across the desk from the farm manager, Tina informed her husband Holmes wished to have a private discussion.

"Certainly, Mr. Holmes," said Everest, sitting back and folding his hands across his brocaded waistcoat. "Did you wish to discuss the Professor?"

Holmes also took up a relaxed position, not wishing to alarm his hosts. He crossed his left ankle over his right knee and also folded his hands across his waist as he answered, "Not precisely, though he may certainly enter into it. Watson and I have just returned from a sojourn about the grounds and found something of which you may not be aware."

Relaying his discovery of the tracks and their location, he enquired, "Has there been any significant change lately? New purchases for example?"

Everest was mulling that over while Tina spoke up, "Certainly we have purchased Christmas gifts, but I cannot imagine any of them being of such value as to make our home a target for burglars."

As she made that statement, her husband made a surreptitious movement indicating that he might have something to share with Holmes privately. Out loud he said, "It's not particularly recent, but we did obtain a new prize breeding bull early last month. It certainly has significant value. Do you think it may be in jeopardy?"

Holmes, tilted his head, "It is far too early to tell what this perpetrator's goal might be. A bull would certainly not be an easy thing to steal, but not impossible. I trust it has been re-branded?"

"Yes, Mr. Holmes we did that the first day we came into possession."

"Does it have any other distinguishing features which might make it easily identifiable from a distance?"

Everest shrugged his shoulders and replied, "Nothing in particular, except perhaps its colour. This one is a South Devon breed and is solid red with no white markings at all. I haven't seen any others like it amongst our neighbour's herds so it would likely stand out."

Holmes seized the opportunity to get Tina's husband alone and suggested that they go out to take a look at it while she returned to her knitting and to tell me to meet them in the barn. Once they were out of earshot of the house, Everest revealed his secret to the detective.

"We are generally not ones for extravagant gifts to each other, Mr. Holmes. We live simple lives and don't engage in multiple social events, being out here in the country. However, we have the most successful farm in the county and the Professor is a well-respected scholar, so we do have occasion, two or three times a year, to attend gatherings that rise above the level of a local barn dance. We own minimal formal wear but can hold our own in fashionable attire. What is missing is any special item of jewellery for Tina with which to adorn herself. Years ago I gave her a five-carat blue topaz pendant, as that is her birthstone, as she was born on Christmas Day. It is a beautiful piece on a simple gold chain. But I wanted her to have an item really worthy of her beauty and my love for her. The farm has done exceptionally well the past two years and shown enough profits for me to obtain something special. I purchased a rare six-strand pearl necklace, crafted with six-millimetre pearls. There is a large blue topaz decorated by surrounding pearls inset into a gold filigree ring, and a pair of waterdrop pearls descending underneath. The jeweller refers to them as the Gemini pearls as they are perfectly matched like twins. That necklace is worth £500. Certainly, a tempting target if anyone is aware of it."

I was just catching up to them by then and heard that final statement. Holmes asked, "Is there anyone in the household aware of it? The Professor, perhaps?"

Everest shook his head, "No, with his mental powers deteriorating I could not trust that he would not inadvertently say something and spoil the surprise. I purchased it on a business trip down to London weeks ago and told no one. I have a separate strong box for my personal papers and valuables which only Tina and I know the combination of and we respect each other's privacy. She would not open it without my permission any more than I would go through her purse without her permission."

"Who was the jeweller who created it?" asked the detective.

"Yakub Goldschmidt of Hatton Garden and before you ask, I had it insured before it ever left the shop."

Holmes nodded in approval, "A wise precaution. Insurance records are kept confidential and the chance of someone learning of your purchase through them is highly unlikely. Jewellers, however, tend to boast of their creations. It is possible that they took a photograph of your piece to show to other potential clients."

Everest nodded, "They did, Mr. Holmes. They even gave me a copy of it to give to my insurance company for their records."

"How much do they know about you?"

We had reached the barn by this time and he opened the door so we could step in out of the cold. Securing it shut, he replied, "The jeweller only knows my surname and that I travel to London occasionally on business. They do not know what type of business I am in, nor my address."

"What information was on the cheque that you paid them with?"

"I paid them in cash, Mr. Holmes, and the receipt was simply made out to 'Mr. Everest'."

Holmes gazed upon what I must now call our client with a nod and the words "Very good."

"My university tutors in bookkeeping emphasised the appropriate amount of detail for any given transaction. In this case, caution and confidentiality were an overriding factor." He stopped and pointed towards a particular stall, "Ah, here is our prize bull, Mr. Holmes. His name is Samson."

Chapter Four

The creature in the stall before us was a magnificent specimen. It was a short horn and red as an Irish Setter. Its height at the shoulder was nearly as tall as my shoulder and Everest told us it weighed over two thousand pounds. As I took in its great size, I wondered aloud at how such a beast is kept under control.

"Fortunately," replied the farm manager, "he was raised on a small family farm where he had human contact every day from the children who cared for him from birth. He's quite tame and appears to have settled in well to his new surroundings. We're not quite ready to have Margie around him, but Tina brushes and speaks to him every day and he seems to understand simple commands to get him to move."

Holmes enquired, "He was not wary of strangers when he arrived?"

Everest smiled, "Oddly enough, only the men. He would alternately draw away from them or charge them. Tina, however, has had no trouble with him at all and he doesn't bother the milkmaids. I suppose it may be their higher-pitched voices, sounding much like the children he was raised with."

Holmes nodded, "That may bode well for us if Samson is the target of your mysterious visitor. He would likely put up a fuss which would rouse the household should someone attempt to lead him away."

"They would be foolish to try," agreed the young man. "The barn is kept locked and if they did breach it, the noise of the animals being disturbed in the middle of the night would certainly draw attention to their presence."

He folded his arms across his chest and asked the detective, "What do you propose we do, Mr. Holmes? Should we set a trap, or post a guard?"

Holmes thought for a moment, then gestured for us to follow him to the barn's entrance. He gazed towards the spot where we had found the tracks, then in the direction of the house. At last, he said over his shoulder to our host, "Have you a telescope?"

Everest hesitated at the oddity of this request, then realised its significance, "Yes, yes, Mr. Holmes, we do."

"I should like to borrow it this evening. Perhaps for several evenings, depending upon our quarry's actions."

"You wish to observe him from a distance?" I enquired, questioningly. "Why not stake out his crossing point and catch him in the act?"

My friend turned to me, "In the act of what, Watson? All we could charge him with is trespassing. He could claim he merely got lost and was trying to obtain his bearings. At most, he would receive a fine and be free again to complete his actual crime. I suggest that we observe him discreetly from a distance and see how close he dares to come, and ascertain whether it be the barn or the house that holds his object of interest."

Everest spoke up, "There is an attic window on this side of the house which would be ideal to observe from. It overlooks the whole property in this direction."

Thus, it was agreed. Starting that evening, one of us would sit up in the attic with the telescope to keep an eye out for any intruder and note their actions. I foresaw one possible obstacle to that plan, however. "Professor Nichols will be expecting us to keep him company in the evenings. Will he not become suspicious if one of us is continually missing? I'm assuming, of course, you wish to keep this possible danger from him, so as to not aggravate his fragile state of mind."

Everest nodded in agreement and turned to my friend, "It would be better if he didn't know, Mr. Holmes. We also need to consider the dinner hour when all of us will be expected to eat together."

Holmes, still looking out upon the pasture, was silent for some moments, then turned his gaze back upon us. "We, of course, must inform Tina, and as I recall she is a very observant person. Is there a trustworthy servant that you could enlist? Someone who would take his meals at a different time than the household without notice?"

Everest immediately answered, "As long as we don't tell Tina about the necklace specifically, just that there is a valuable item on the farm. I would still like to keep that a surprise. Young Donny McCallum could assist us. You may remember his father, Donald, was the dairy foreman back when you visited before. He passed away some four years ago. The medical condition that had forced him to give up his navy career and take up farming finally caught up with him. His son, Donald, is nineteen now and has grown up here. He is a natural with the animals and treats them like his own. A stalwart lad. I'm sure we can trust him."

At this point, a loud 'Halloa' emanated from the front porch as Professor Nichols came out to seek us. Everest returned his call and waved. As the Professor crossed the fifty-yard distance between us, our client spoke softly, "I'll speak to Donny and arrange everything in the attic. When you go up to dress for dinner, I'll show you the way to its entrance."

Nichols soon reached us, only slightly winded from his effort, "Well, boys," he said, "admiring our new prize bull? A beauty, isn't he?"

"Indeed, Professor," replied my companion. "A fine-looking animal. He should prove most conducive to the expansion of your herd."

The elderly man beamed and put a hand on Everest's shoulder, "Yes business is doing quite well, thanks to Noel here. I was lucky my daughter found such a prize herself."

The young man blushed at the praise and replied, "Our guests were just getting ready to return. I've a few things to speak to Donny about, then I'll join you shortly."

We retreated to the house maintaining a slow pace in deference to the Professor. Once inside and divested from our outerwear, he suggested a trip down into the cellar and a round of target practice. I offered to retrieve our guns from our rooms while Holmes accompanied his former instructor down the stairs. When I rejoined them, Nichols was showing off a new item from his collection.

"Ah, Doctor!" cried the gun enthusiast as I came through the door at the bottom of the steps. "You are just in time. Come and take a look at this."

I joined them by the shooting bench and set down the cases containing the Colts the Professor had given us all those years ago. He handed me a lever-action rifle with a polished brass receiver and beautifully grained walnut stock. The lever was already opened revealing an empty breech. It was quite a bit shorter than the Martini-Henry rifle I was familiar with during my army service, but the weight appeared about the same. As I hefted it into a firing position, Nichols expounded upon the details.

"It's an American Henry Rifle, first produced in 1860 by the New Haven Arms Company. Revolutionary for its time with a fifteen-round tubular magazine plus one in the chamber, firing .44 calibre rimfire cartridges. In spite of this greater capacity over the standard single-shot rifles, during the Civil War, the Union Army purchased less than two thousand because of its lack of a bayonet. It's widely believed, however, that some six or seven thousand made their way into battle through purchases by individual soldiers who felt the greater firepower would save their lives. A Confederate Colonel, John Mosby, once cursed it as 'that damned Yankee rifle that can be loaded on Sunday and fired all week'."

Holmes spoke up, "What is the effective range of this weapon?"

Nichols smiled, "The manufacturer claims over four hundred yards, but I've read a good many articles on weapons and my research indicates it loses accuracy at anything over two hundred."

Holmes walked over to the gun case and picked out another ancient long gun. "I believe this Girandoni air rifle has a range of one hundred and fifty yards, does it not? May I fire a few rounds?"

"Certainly, Sherlock, but I must warn you that the capacity is currently only about ten rounds. It takes fifteen hundred strokes of the air pump to power its thirty maximum shots. The main reason for its discontinuation. Though I do have a spare, fully charged air container like the ones the Austrian army used."

Nichols reached for a box of cartridges and handed them to me, "Here, Doctor. Give the Henry a try."

The steel plate backdrop for his firing range was some sixty feet from the firing line as it ran nearly the length of the house with support beams in neat rows. Certainly, the distance was no challenge for the rifles and muskets in his collection. I loaded and stepped up next to Holmes who was proving quite proficient with the air rifle. The Henry proved to be well-sighted in and I obliterated the centre ring of the target I had chosen with just six shots. I handed it back to Nichols saying, "A most proficient weapon. I can see why Union soldiers would pay their own money for it."

I looked towards the gun cases I had brought down, "How are your pistol skills, Professor? Care to compete with those Colts you gave us?"

I opened the cases to reveal two matched 1873 Colt Peacemaker, single action revolvers with seven-and-one-half inch barrels for greater accuracy. These were nickel-plated with ivory handles; disturbingly beautiful for something so deadly.

Nichols picked one up gingerly, running his fingers along its long barrel before taking up a firing position to test its heft. "Ah, these are beauties indeed! I hope you and Sherlock have been putting them to good use in your pursuit of justice."

I did not have the heart to tell him that we rarely used them. Usually, when we went out armed it was with concealment in mind and my army Webley and Holmes's five-inch Bulldog were much easier to fit into our pockets. He checked the cylinder and saw the hammer was on an empty chamber but the rest were loaded. He picked out a target and, using a two-handed stance, slowly put five shots into it.

"Excellent, Professor!" declared Holmes, seeing a tight pattern upon the bullseye. "Watson, I believe that you've met your match this time."

I gave my friend a look, for my skills were certainly equal to the task of repeating Nichols's feat. Then I saw the countenance on my friend's face and realised what he was saying. I took up my stance and deliberately put three of my shots on the outer rim of the centre circle. This pleased the elderly man no end and gave me more satisfaction in making him happy than winning a match ever could.

We continued in this manner, testing various weapons in his collection. When at last the dinner hour was approaching, Holmes asked a question, "Professor, would you mind if I took the Girandoni for some outdoor shooting tomorrow? I'd like to test it over a longer range."

"By all means, Sherlock. Be my guest."

Chapter Five

Everest joined us at the bottom of the stairs as we prepared to ascend them to change for dinner. He led us up to the attic where we were met by a handsome young lad, nearly six feet tall yet lean as a rail. He sported long blond hair, a moustache, and the beginnings of a beard. At our introduction, he greeted us enthusiastically, "I've read your stories, Dr. Watson and I must say, it is an honour to meet you, Mr. Holmes. I should be happy to assist in any way I can."

"Thank you, Mr. McCallum," the detective replied. "For now, your task will be strictly observation and reporting, though there may come a time when your physical assistance may be called upon."

"Anything you say, sir" answered the lad. "We've set the telescope up over here. I've kept it back from the window so it can't be spotted by anyone far away. I'll also keep the lantern low and behind this trunk so there won't appear to be any light emanating from this window. There will be just enough though so that we can see our way in and out of the room."

Holmes stepped over to the telescope and sat upon the chair behind it. He peered through the lens and made a slight adjustment. "Very good. That is the exact spot where we observed the tracks coming to a stop." Then he noted a pair of field glasses on a box next to the chair. Everest offered, "I thought that those might come in handy as well. We can use them to scan the area in case the trespasser comes by a different route. That way we won't have to move the telescope and try to find our way back to the location in the dark."

Holmes stood and rubbed his palms together, "Excellent, Mr. Everest! Your foresight may prove fortuitous. What time does the Professor usually retire?"

The Manager answered, "Generally he retires no later than ten o'clock, but with your presence, he may be inspired to stay up later."

Holmes nodded thoughtfully, "I believe that we can come up with an excuse for either Watson or I to be off to bed by that time, should it prove necessary. Mr. McCallum, I presume that you will eat your dinner early enough to be here by dusk?"

"Easily done, sir"

"Excellent! One of us will relieve you by ten o'clock or sooner. I think that we can cease our watch by midnight. This intruder is still in reconnoitring mode and is not likely to take any action for a day or two at least. If it is the house he watches, it will probably be only as long as the lights are on."

"Begging your pardon, Mr. Holmes," said the young lad, "How do you know that?"

Holmes indulged the boy with his logic, "Our observation reveals that he has only looked upon the farm once from that spot which provides the best concealment. Whatever he is planning will require at least two or three days of scouting to learn the ways of the household before he strikes. Someone with the foresight to obscure his tracks will not act impulsively. They will plan their action carefully and that gives us time."

With tactics thus set, we prepared ourselves and joined the family for dinner. Discussion of the upcoming holiday was lively, especially the charming conversation carried on by young Marjorie. She had quite an extensive list of things she was hoping to receive, especially concerning her doll's house family.

"They need a barn with animals to be a proper country squire and family," she declared in as authoritative a voice as a four-year-old can muster.

Her father, in mock seriousness, asked, "What if the father wishes to be a barrister, or a merchant, or an actor? Then they would live in town, wouldn't they?"

She looked at him with wide blue eyes and a shocked expression, "No, these are *my* family. The father is a country squire. Nothing is better than that!"

Noel chose not to argue and her grandfather, Professor Nichols, reached over and tousled her hair, "That's right, child. But a man can be many things in his life. I was a university professor before I became a dairy farmer."

"But being a country squire must be better, or you would still be a professor!" she replied with her innocent reasoning.

Knowing better than to argue with a four-year-old's logic, Nichols changed the subject and addressed my friend, "So, Sherlock, how was your walk this afternoon? Did you find any good fishing spots?"

Holmes politely shook his head, "I am afraid that the stream is frozen over too thickly. But, tell me, Professor, I know the woods across it are open for public use, how large a forest is that?"

Nichols pursed his lips and looked down in thought, "Oh, it's about four miles north to south and varies in width from half a mile to a mile."

Holmes feigned surprise. I knew he already had this information and I was wondering where this line of questioning was going. "That large? I suppose that creates a natural barrier between you and your western neighbour."

"Hatherly's farm? Indeed, it does. Not that it matters. He's a good neighbour. Mostly vegetable crops at his place. Broccoli, Brussels sprouts, and the like. We occasionally trade milk for vegetables with him."

"Have you ever had any of your cattle wander over there?"

"Never" answered Nichols. "Our livestock are content to remain on our side of the stream. There's nothing for them to eat in the woods and Hatherley's crops are too far away to attract them."

"I suppose the woods are open to hunters, so it's probably just as well your cattle do not wander through them."

119

"We have an ordinance about that, Sherlock. No rifles are allowed in those woods. Hunting may only be done by shotguns using birdshot, or archery. Wouldn't want some stray bullet finding its way onto our pastures."

"A wise precaution," replied the detective.

The subject changed to more pleasant topics and little Marjorie was regaled with stories of Christmases past. After dinner, Holmes and the Professor retreated to his study where Nichols insisted on showing Holmes his latest research, while Everest and I took up a game of billiards.

As the hour approached ten o'clock the farm manager and I quit our game, stuck our heads into the study to say goodnight, and proceeded upstairs. In the attic, we found that Tina had replaced young Donny after she had lain Margie down to sleep. She reported no sign of anyone and I volunteered to take her place to allow her to join Noel for a nightcap. I was wide awake and knew that Holmes would likely be up shortly.

I settled into the chair and peered through the telescope fixed on the spot where we had observed the culprit's tracks. Nothing was to be seen there. Thus, I took up the field glasses and did a quick surveillance of the surrounding area. To quote an appropriate poem for the season, 'Not a creature was stirring'. I was just about to set the glasses aside when Holmes arrived. To my surprise, he was carrying the Girandoni air rifle. "Do you think that will be necessary, Holmes? You certainly can't shoot a man on sight just for trespassing."

He set the gun aside and replied, "Just a precaution, old friend. It is best to be prepared for any contingency. Just as I would advise you to keep your Webley at hand should we have to pursue our quarry."

"Well, our friend has yet to show himself this evening," I said, handing him the binoculars. "All seems quiet, so far."

I again took up my view through the telescope. It was well that the moon was heading into its full phase over the next few days and the sky only held scattered clouds, making for a bright view of the pastureland that we were watching. As I heard the distant chime of a clock somewhere in the house announcing ten-thirty, Holmes suddenly stood and appeared to adjust the focus on the lenses of the field glasses. "We have movement, Watson," he said in a low voice. "Someone is crossing the stream at the same spot we noted earlier today."

I made a slight adjustment to the telescope and spotted a figure gingerly crossing the ice. They were well wrapped up against the cold so that I could not make out much of their physicality. The face was covered by a muffler and a beaver hat with earflaps was pulled low on their brow. Assuming the bulk of their body was caused by the heavy coat, it appeared that they were of average size, certainly not obese. I couldn't judge their height from this far away until they got to the same mound of rocks that we had been to earlier that day. Standing next to them, they appeared much shorter than I – perhaps five foot five inches but possibly less, depending on their boot heels.

Suddenly, as they pulled out a pair of field glasses, Holmes said, "Get back, Watson! Step to the side quickly!"

I did as he ordered, stepping out of the line of sight. As I did so, he stealthily reached over and tilted the telescope upward, then ducked out of sight backing into the dark recesses of the attic. Being well away from the window he raised his binoculars again and trained his focus on the spy in the pasture.

"What is it, Holmes?" I asked. "Why did you have me move?"

"I nearly made a blunder, my friend. I suddenly realised that the position of the moon, while being bright enough for us to see them, was also lighting up this side of the house. I noticed the reflection of the telescope lens shining on the window where our nocturnal visitor might have seen it."

"They have not reacted?" I asked, hopefully.

"Fortunately, no," he replied. "Their concentration seems to be on the house rather than the barn, but they appear to be looking at the lower floors. Ah!" he cried, lowering the binoculars and stepping back, "Now they are observing the upper half of the house."

He took a peek and again raised the instrument to his eyes and murmured, "They are writing something down. Now they are leaving the same way they came, again they are stepping in their own tracks." He stood up to full height and said with resolve, "Come along, Doctor. We should examine this new trespass while it is still fresh."

Chapter Six

We donned our overcoats and, accompanied by Everest, we plodded over to the spot. Holmes made sure that our host and I stayed on the side of the pile of rocks towards the house, so as not to leave tracks where the intruder might spot them if he came back again.

This time Holmes was able to find one footprint that the trespasser had failed to smudge and measured it with his pocket tape. "A size seven boot," he said for our benefit. "That would tally with their approximate height. Unfortunately, it does not help us determine if it is a man or woman."

Everest reacted to that, "You think it could be a woman?" he asked with some incredulity. "How often have you run into female burglars, Mr. Holmes?"

Holmes broke a branch off a nearby bush and used it to remove his own tracks in the snow as he answered, "More often than you might think. Their smaller size allows them access to spaces where one would not normally expect an entrance. They also use their gender to attend parties and move about more freely, or to obtain positions within a household until they can accomplish their mission."

"Well, we certainly aren't planning on hiring anyone and we are not hosting any parties, though we will be attending one on Christmas Eve and another on New Year's Eve."

"I assume that Tina will be wearing the necklace on both those occasions."

"I expect she will. I am giving it to her on Christmas Eve so that she can wear it to the Christmas extravaganza in Oxford that night. Then there will be the local M.P.'s New Year's Eve ball in Aylesbury."

Holmes nodded, then said, "Why don't you go back to the house and get some sleep? I want to cross the stream and see how far I can follow these tracks to ascertain which direction they go in. Watson, I would welcome your company if your leg is up to it."

In truth, my old war wound was acting up with the cold, but I was not about to leave my friend to face an unknown intruder alone. "I'll come with you, Holmes. Lead on."

We crossed the stream's solid ice and emerged on the other side. The full moon illuminated the ground for a while, but once into the shade of the trees, Holmes was forced to use his bullseye lantern and direct the light downward to keep it from giving our position away. The tracks did not go directly through the woods towards Nichols's neighbour to the west, but rather turned northwards. We had not gone very far when we found a spot with fresh horse tracks and signs of our visitor mounting and riding through the woods until they reached the main road. From that point, the traffic made the tracks impossible to follow.

Once back at the house and standing before a warm fire with a cup of tea before retiring, I asked my companion, "If this person is observing the house, Holmes, shouldn't they be doing so from more than one side?"

"Yes, Watson," he replied. "Tomorrow we shall have to walk the perimeter again and see if there are other signs of their incursion. I doubt that they could infiltrate from the south as the land is sparse with no hiding places. But the road from Aylesbury that circles the northern boundary and then turns south along the eastern side of the property may provide them with some observation points."

"Observing from the road seems rather risky," I noted.

"During daylight with traffic, certainly," replied Holmes. "But at night there are ways that they could manage it."

Aylesbury, being the county town of Buckinghamshire had well-paved roads throughout the surrounding area, thus, they were used frequently throughout the winter. During our sojourn the next day, Holmes found signs along the roadside of where a horse had left the macadam surface and stopped in the mud perhaps one hundred and fifty yards due east of Nichols's house. The tracks were easy to spot as they had run into the snow shovelled to the side of the road.

"These appear to have been made last night, Watson. Perhaps after our late-night visitor left his lookout on the west side. See how the hardened snow has cracked from the weight of the horse. It had already frozen from the cold night air."

Holmes turned his gaze toward Nichols's home and found that, from that vantage point, the top of the barn was barely visible above the roofline of the house. He pointed in that direction so I could follow his gaze, "I believe that we can now be fairly certain that our trespasser was reconnoitring the house, Doctor. That at least narrows the targets of whatever crime they are looking to commit."

"So, what now, Holmes?" I asked

The detective stroked his chin in thought, then replied, "I have some further enquiries to make of the family, then I shall have to smoke a pipe or two upon the matter. Tomorrow is Christmas Eve and the necklace shall make its first public appearance so we must make our plans today."

The enquiries that Holmes made were to Tina, to see if she had purchased anything of significance in the way of Christmas gifts for her family, and to Noel to ensure that the Professor had not come into possession of some valuable object related to his academic work. Neither proved to be the case. The only other recent purchase of significant value was that of the red bull. Thus, the pearl necklace remained the most likely target for a thief.

Holmes, as was his habit when upon a case, shut himself away in his room with a good supply of tobacco and his pipe. He did make an appearance at lunch so as not to alarm the Professor by his absence, but he ate sparingly as he always refuses to be distracted by digestion when contemplating a problem.

Finally, just before tea time, Holmes asked me to bring Everest up to his room for a conference. When we had all settled into place, Holmes, leaning on the window sill, began to explain his thoughts and plan of action.

"I have attempted to put myself in our potential thief's place," he began. "Were I the one planning to steal this necklace, I would take much more time and many more steps to glean information and wait until such a time as most of the family is away without taking the necklace with them. Then I would have no need to subject myself to the cold weather of late winter nights as this person has done. I would attempt to infiltrate the social gatherings where it would be worn and see what information I might overhear about where it is kept or on what occasions it is to be worn. I might attempt to become a casual worker on the estate during the spring when there is much more work to be done. Or, if it is a woman, to arrange to replace one of the milkmaids.

"However, as this person is spending the time to do their surveying now and under these adverse conditions, I can only assume that they mean to attempt their crime in the near future.

"That said, I believe that their greatest chance for success lies not in burgling the house, but in highway robbery while you are traveling either to or from the train station during your Oxford trip tomorrow, or while on the road into town for the New Year's Eve Ball."

My friend paused and let that sink in. Everest, after a momentary hesitation to process this fact, gazed up at him and asked, "What do you propose we do to stop them? Should I hire some men for the trip?"

Holmes shook his head, "A show of force will discourage them, certainly. However, it is my recommendation that we take another tack and catch them in the act once and for all so that we might put your worries to rest."

Holmes laid out his plan adding, "I believe that their ideal opportunity would be to confront you on the road home after the Oxford trip. The lateness of the hour would ensure no other traffic on the road and a significant delay in your getting to town and stirring up the constabulary to pursue them. Let me suggest this …"

He went on to outline his ideas and after a discussion, we all agreed as to our roles and its execution.

Chapter Seven

That evening we were all treated to a recital by Tina on the piano and Margie, who was learning the basics of the violin from her mother. I recalled that Holmes had informed me during our first visit to Nichols that Tina's mother was an excellent musician and had taught her daughter both the piano and violin before her untimely death when Tina was nine.

Christmas Eve dawn broke with blue skies and scattered white clouds with no sign of rain or snow. We spent the day dressing the tree as the Professor and the Everests were going to be gone that night to Oxford. Margie was filled with excitement and squealed with delight when her father presented Tina with the Gemini pearl necklace after lunch. Tina was taken aback by the extravagance of her gift.

"Noel, it's beautiful," she said. "But ..."

He cut her off, "But nothing. It's no less than you deserve, my Love, and I wanted you to have something to show off at Oxford."

She hugged him and replied, "I have the finest husband in all Aylesbury. That's all I need to be the envy of every woman at both Oxford and the New Year's Eve Ball."

Needless to say, compliments volleyed back and forth between the couple, the Professor, and the rest of us. Soon it was time to get ready for the ride into town to catch the late afternoon train to Oxford. Holmes remained in close proximity to the family as we had agreed. I stayed at the farm with the staff to protect Margie and the house in case we were wrong about the target of those espying the farm. Donny McCallum was given a rifle and was instructed to stand guard at the barn with other farmhands, and both Clinton, the butler, and I discreetly armed ourselves in case of a break-in. While remaining diligent, I still was able to have a delightful time watching over Margie, telling stories, and playing games. It was a double-edged sword in that she was an adorable child and yet, still a reminder of the fact that my Mary had died before we could start our own family. I am afraid I let my feelings give in to the child's persistence for 'one more story' before I finally put her to bed, a half-hour past her usual bedtime.

I took up my post in the attic, searching the grounds to the west, while Clinton remained downstairs watching the eastern side of the estate while making rounds of all the ground floor doors every half an hour. The night was clear and still, befitting the Christmas carol, *Silent Night.*

It was not so, however, for Professor Nichols and the Everests.

The drive into Aylesbury to catch the Oxford-bound train was without incident. The enclosed carriage was comfortable and the travelling rugs kept the passengers warm against the late afternoon chill.

Likewise, the train ran on schedule and all arrived sufficiently early to attend a delightful evening at the Oxford extravaganza, a combination of student exhibits, musical performances, and ballroom dancing. Professor Nichols was welcomed enthusiastically by several faculty members and Tina's necklace was much remarked upon.

They caught the last train out of Oxford and arrived in Aylesbury just before midnight. The driver they had engaged for the evening was a one-armed man who was expert at the Hungarian rein style of using just his good left hand to drive the carriage while his right sleeve hung empty, tucked into his coat pocket. There had been some concern expressed over this, as there may be a need to whip up the horse for a fast getaway, but it was Christmas Eve and most of the staff had been given that evening and the next day off to celebrate the season.

The moon was still nearly full on a cloudless night making for excellent visibility. Noel Everest kept watch of the countryside out of the window in anticipation of what Holmes feared. Though he knew the detective was close by, the anticipation of danger still jangled his nerves. Just as they were passing the edge of the forest that ran south along the western border of the farm, the carriage was reined to a stop, and a voice from the opposite side to where Everest had been watching called out, "Stop right there or I'll blow your bloody head off!"

The driver might have been willing to snap the reins and make a run for it had he been alone, but he was not willing to risk a shot coming from behind that might strike one of his passengers so he pulled up.

This highway robber was a muscular fellow though not very tall. A black bandana covered the lower half of his face and a shotgun filled his hands. He shouted out, "Everybody out! Now! You," he shouted at the driver, "get down here and don't try no funny business."

Speaking to all he said, "Gentlemen, I'll have your wallets if you please. Then, staring at Tina, his eyes narrowed, "And you, m'lady, just open up that coat of yours, and let's see what pretty baubles might be hangin' about your neck."

The Professor started to protest but Noel put a hand upon his shoulder, and said, "Just do as he says, Professor."

The men reached for their wallets inside their coats as Tina undid the clasp and buttons on her coat. When she pulled the lapels apart to reveal her neckline, the robber gasped, lowering his shotgun as he stepped closer saying, "What the bloody hell?"

She was no longer wearing the necklace and that element of surprise was enough to distract the bandit. Suddenly, instead of pulling out his wallet, Noel drew a pepper-box revolver with its two- and one-half inch barrel that fitted neatly into his breast pocket and shot the robber in the shoulder, forcing him to drop his gun. At the same time, the one-armed driver came up with a British Bull Dog revolver in the right arm hidden under his coat and fired as well. Sherlock Holmes, as the driver in disguise, had shot the man near his hip, forcing him to fall to the ground.

Though we in the house must have been over a mile from this incident, the shots echoed over the fields. Knowing now that the trouble was out on the road I charged out to the barn and mounted a horse that had already been saddled in the event that we had to ride to fetch the police. Donny left the barn and joined Clinton in the house to maintain guard there while I goaded the animal into a gallop across the northern pasture towards the sound of the gunfire.

I spotted the carriage lamps and approached quickly, my old army Webley in hand in case of trouble. Fortunately, I found everyone healthy save for one rogue lying on the floor of the carriage as he was to be transported back to town for treatment, arrest, and questioning. Holmes and Everest had staunched the bleeding, neither having hit any significant artery. I examined him quickly and though wounded and in pain, the man was in no immediate danger.

After arriving at the local police station at close to one o'clock we arranged for a solitary cell away from the Christmas Eve drunkards and I treated the fellow's injuries more thoroughly, removing the bullets and stitching the wounds with supplies from the police surgeon's office, while an Inspector Albertson was briefed by Sherlock Holmes. He was a wizened old veteran of the police force. Roughly five foot ten inches tall and fifty years of age he was still in good physical condition having not allowed age to let his muscular chest sink into a fat belly. He regularly walked the streets of Aylesbury to check on his men, thus keeping his legs in peak condition for chasing down miscreants. His moustache had turned grey but his hair was still thick and light brown, and his eyes as keen as a hawk's.

The Inspector listened with great interest but replied somewhat piqued at the actions Holmes had taken. "You should have let us know what was going on, Mr. Holmes. We could have offered protection. The Professor and the Everests are among our leading citizens."

Holmes smiled indulgently, "All I had was speculation based upon rudimentary deductions, Inspector. I could not be sure that they would strike tonight and you, I am sure, had your hands full policing the town on this night of celebrations. This way, by seeming to be unguarded, we drew him into a trap and captured him in the act."

"So where is this necklace he was after?"

Holmes unpinned the empty sleeve of his jacket and pulled the necklace from the pocket. "Safe and sound. I knew that the sight of Mrs. Everest not wearing the actual object of his act would cause a moment of hesitation. Mr. Everest and I had agreed that was when we would take action."

Albertson examined the mass of pearls and handed it to Tina, "I'll not deprive you of your Christmas gift at this time, Mrs. Everest. But bear in mind that we will need it as evidence for the trial."

"Thank you, Inspector. We shall take great care of it," she answered, handing it to her husband to fasten about her neck once again.

After taking their statements, Albertson allowed me to drive the family back to the farm while I left my horse for Holmes to follow when he was finished. He still had many questions for this hijacker before he could be satisfied that the danger had passed.

Chapter Eight

Upon a search a short letter was found addressed to 'Parson Donner, Morrisey Inn, Aylesbury'. The fact that Donner's first name could be confused for an occupational title apparently had served him well in not being suspected often during his criminal career. But this time he had been caught red-handed. The essence of the missive was that he should proceed as discussed upon the return of the 'object' on the night of the twenty-fourth at the place planned upon. The 'object' was then be transported to London on the twenty-fifth and delivered for payment at the previous meeting place at three o'clock.

Cryptic as it was meant to be, should it have been discovered before the crime, now that it was found in Donner's possession after being caught, the meaning was quite clear. He was not acting on his own but as the agent of another higher-up. That meant further danger for the Everests if this mastermind was not deterred for good.

Donner was still a little groggy from the painkillers I had given him while removing the bullets from his shoulder and hip, but he was awake enough to answer questions. Especially after Inspector Albertson told him his only chance of leniency was to name his accomplice.

"What sort of leniency?" asked the criminal.

"That will be up to the Crown Prosecutor. But it could be a reduced sentence."

Donner shook his head, trying to clear the effects of the pain and medication. Finally, he replied, "Well, it weren't my idea, I can tell you that. I'll be glad to tell his name. It'll serve him right for getting me into this spot."

When he gave out his partner's identity, Holmes nodded with satisfaction and replied, "I suspected as much."

"Who is that, Mr. Holmes?" asked Albertson.

"One of the few men who knew of the necklace's existence before tonight, Inspector."

When next I saw Holmes, we were opening presents on Christmas morning. Margie was admiring the additional items for her doll's house and all were in good spirits. My friend appeared in the doorway of the great room and was immediately pounced upon by the young girl who thanked him for the present he had left her under the tree, a book of elementary violin music. The adults, of course, were all anxious to hear what had transpired at the police station but did not wish to discuss it in front of the child. At Tina's urging, Margie went off to assist Mrs. Ricciardo in the kitchen, as playtime was not to occur until after a breakfast of thanksgiving for the holiday.

Once she was out of earshot, Holmes described what he had learned and what steps he and Inspector Albertson were about to take. Noel was incensed when he learned who the author of the crime was and wanted to join us, but my friend dissuaded him by suggesting that his place was with his family on this holy day, and that this type of work was best left to himself and the police.

Inspector Albertson insisted on accompanying us back to London. Having been denied the capture of Donner, he was not about to be left out of the arrest of the intellect behind the attempted theft. We were met in London by Inspector Stanley Hopkins, a frequent Scotland Yard cohort during those latter years of the 19th century.

Despite Hopkins being nearly equal to Holmes's height, thus being several inches taller than Albertson, and being assigned directly to Scotland Yard, the younger Inspector bowed in deference to his elder counterpart. Both officials allowed Holmes to present his plans for the capture of our quarry and agreed to his proposal.

The meeting place for the rendezvous was a Jewish café on Brick Lane in Spitalfields. It was one of the few places open on Christmas Day, and attracted the lower classes of London's gentiles who had no place or no one with whom to celebrate Christmas. This lent itself to both the criminal's purpose and our own. Donner would not seem out of place meeting his employer, nor would those of our party who would be on hand to observe the exchange.

Fortunately, Holmes's shot to Donner's hip had struck only flesh so my removal of the bullet and stitching was sufficient to allow him to walk with only a minor limp. His right arm, however, was forced to be in a sling from his shoulder wound. At three o'clock Donner entered using an old bamboo cane provided by Holmes. It was sufficient to hold his weight but should he attempt to use it as a weapon it would easily be broken. I had gone in earlier and watched from a table across the room while others were in less conspicuous locations. He spotted the man who had hired him and made for the table, which was situated by the kitchen door.

He sank heavily into the seat opposite and immediately the man sitting there looked upon him with concern. He was Jewish in appearance and nearing thirty years of age with curly black hair under his yarmulke and a medium-length black beard. He immediately questioned our prisoner, *sotto voce*, "What happened? Did you get the necklace?"

In answer Donner pulled a leather pouch from inside his sling and dropped it on the table, giving off the distinct sound of several round objects clacking together. "I had a bit of trouble with the husband. He tried to shoot it out with me. Suffice to say, one of us lost," he said with a wink.

"You killed him?" cried our quarry, fighting to keep his voice low. "How? No one was supposed to get hurt!"

"The farm was too well guarded for a burglary," replied Donner. "I had to use our secondary plan and go for a robbery instead. I got your merchandise. Now where's my money?"

The young Jew pulled an envelope from his inner breast pocket and set it on the table in front of him. He then reached for the leather pouch but Donner reached out with his good hand and stopped him. "Let's see what's in the envelope first."

The lad, clearly shaken by the thought that the theft had turned into murder, nervously looked about the room. There were too many strangers. He began to re-think his choice of meeting places and shook his head, "Not here, follow me."

He stood and stepped towards the kitchen. Donner hesitated, looked around, and then followed. I moved across the room to stand by the kitchen door to prevent a return to the dining area. Once behind the closed door, Donner's employer made his way in the direction of the back door that led to the alley. It became obvious that his purpose was to make the exchange and beat a hasty retreat. In a quiet corner, he stopped and opened the envelope enough for Donner to see his fee. The thief held out the leather pouch and they exchanged the items simultaneously.

Suddenly a voice spoke out in a lecturing tone, "You should have asked to see the necklace before handing over the money, Mr. Goldschmidt."

The young man spun around as a tall chef removed his hat and approached him holding up a small revolver. "My name is Sherlock Holmes and you are under arrest."

Goldschmidt gasped, took a quick look in the bag to find that it was merely full of marbles, then flung it at Holmes and lunged for the back door. Upon opening it, however, he was greeted by Inspector Hopkins and two uniformed constables. The Inspector quickly subdued and handcuffed the culprit while Holmes and I escorted Donner out of the door, rather than back through the restaurant. We all then came back around to the front through a side alley to rejoin Inspector Albertson, who had dropped off his prisoner at the beginning of this meeting.

Back at Scotland Yard Hopkins locked up Donner and allowed Albertson and Holmes to do the questioning of Anan Goldschmidt, brother of Yakub Goldschmidt, the jeweler who had sold the Gemini necklace. I stood by taking notes of the interrogation.

Albertson started by asking the obvious, "Does your brother know about this? Did he help you plan it?"

Anan, with his head down, shook it slowly, and said bitterly, "No, no, no. Yakub was not involved. He knows nothing of this."

"Then how did you find out about the necklace and where Noel Everest lived?"

"I work part-time at the stop. I was the one who worked on the piece and I overheard my brother and Everest talking about the weather for there was heavy snow the day he picked it up. He mentioned that in Aylesbury the storm had passed south of them. So, I had a last name and a location. It took some time and a few well-spent coins, but I eventually found out where he lived."

Holmes spoke up, "Your crime appears to have been rushed. Why were you in such a hurry that you chose to go after the necklace at this time instead of taking longer to plan something with a greater chance of success?"

The young man buried his face in his trembling hands and mumbled, "I owe money to some impatient people, who are not above physical threats to collect. They demanded repayment before the New Year."

"Why involve Donner?" asked Albertson.

Holmes replied for the prisoner, "Look at his hands, Inspector."

Anan dropped his hands to the tabletop where they continued to shake despite his holding them together. Albertson gazed upon them and then asked, "You have a medical condition?"

He nodded, "'Essential tremors' the doctors say. It comes and goes but I never know when, which is why my brother only lets me work part-time. I couldn't trust myself to sneak into a house and open a safe, and I certainly wouldn't attempt to hold a gun on someone. I've known Donner ever since I caught him trying to pick my pocket several years ago. I knew that I could trust him to play his part for a share of the profit, as I know enough about him to report him to the police if I ever had a mind to do so. I had learned enough information around town to discover the Professor's connection to Oxford and learned of the extravaganza. I returned to London to ensure that I had an alibi should I ever be suspected. When Donner informed me that a burglary was impossible, I wrote back to him saying that their late return from Oxford would be the ideal time for a robbery on the lonely road. Donner kept an eye on the Everests to make sure that the lady was wearing the necklace that night when they left on the train. Then it was just a matter of waiting for their return. We felt sure that they would not spend the night in Oxford with a child awaiting Christmas morning at home. I don't know how you managed to gain the advantage on Donner unless it was because his gun was only meant to scare you."

"What do you mean?" asked the Inspector. "I unloaded that gun myself. He could have killed someone!"

"The shells were supposed to be loaded with rock salt. If necessary, he would have fired a warning shot. We did not expect the Everests or the Professor to go out armed while in their formal wear."

"Just one more question," said Holmes. "Why did you not go to your brother for assistance? Surely the profits of the jewellery stop have made him a wealthy man."

"A wealthy miser, you mean! He may be my brother, but Yakub has had everything handed to him as the eldest son." Anan spat, "Eldest son my eye! *Yimach shmo!*[1] He's my twin and is older than me by only six minutes! He was always set to take over the jewellery business, but never learned to be a jeweller. He's merely a salesman with a talent for management. He pays others to do the work, whereas our father insisted that I had to learn the actual craft of jewellery-making. *I'm* the one with the talent! I was the one with the creative artistry to make that necklace to Everest's design. Yet Yakub takes the profits and pays his workers piecemeal. I was going to pay my debt and

---

[1] Hebrew curse meaning 'May his name be erased!'.

with enough left over to get out from under Yakub's thumb and go and start my own shop abroad."

Albertson replied, "The only place you'll be going for a while is prison."

The jeweller sunk his face into his folded arms on the table in despair while Holmes, the Inspector, and I left him to contemplate his fate. Once outside I commented, "One could almost feel sorry for the fellow. He must have been truly desperate."

Albertson replied, "Many criminals are desperate, Doctor. Or they're too lazy to do honest work, or they're just plain evil. The law is the law and the victims must have satisfaction."

"Will he get the same punishment as Donner, who actually committed the crime?" I asked.

Albertson nodded, "It all falls under an act of conspiracy. He's just lucky no one got hurt other than his co-conspirator. He and Donner will likely get the same sentence."

The law, however, did differentiate between the two men. Donner, as a repeat offender, was sentenced to five years hard labour. Goldschmidt was given a three-year sentence and his medical condition allowed him to serve in a more sedentary capacity. When he was released, Holmes arranged an introduction to a jeweller in Amsterdam where Anan Goldschmidt still works to this day.

Professor Nichols, I am sorry to report, passed away in the spring following this adventure. Noel and Tina Everest still run the dairy farm and Marjorie, though only in her teenage-aged years as of this writing, is performing virtuoso violin concerts in the local theatres.

Cancer: The Crab
(21st June – 22nd July)

The Case of the

One-Armed Crabbe

Passionate but uncommunicative. Behind the brooding fortress that a Cancer has erected to protect themselves are abundant reserves of deep, undying love and loyalty. Pity that few will get to experience it because they aren't the best at communicating what is in their hearts.

Chapter One

It was the end of the 'worst of times', if I may borrow a phrase from Charles Dickens. The Great War was over at last. But Europe had been decimated by millions of deaths counting military and civilians. In addition to those killed by the horrible weapons of war, some two-and-a-half million fell victim to the Spanish flu pandemic of 1918. The total figures may never be known but the last estimate I had heard was that, in total, over five percent of the European population, much of it in the prime of youth, was wiped out in four-and-a-half years.

The Spanish flu, of course, is a misnomer. At the time it occurred, Spain was a neutral country while most of Europe was at war, thus it was the only nation reporting deaths caused by the pandemic. None of the warring countries wanted their enemies to know what losses they were enduring to this terrible disease. It would all come out eventually, but for Sherlock Holmes and me, it was quite evident. We both knew friends who had succumbed to this blight.

It was now summer in the year of our Lord 1920. Only two months before, I had joined Holmes on a commission from his brother Mycroft, to examine the security measures at Chequers[1], the new country home of the Prime Minister. I had been visiting him at the time in his Sussex cottage where he

---

[1] See *The Game at Chequers* in *Sherlock Holmes and the Seven Deadly Sins* by Roger Riccard and published by Baker Street Studios Limited in 2024.

kept bees. Now I was back in London, dividing my time between organising my old case notes on the adventures that Holmes and I had shared, and making house calls upon disabled war veterans whom I had helped to treat upon their return from what would hopefully be the war to end all wars.

One such patient was former Sergeant Thomas Crabbe, a member of an army tank crew tasked with capturing the Amiens railway line stretching between Mericourt and Hangest in August 1918.[1] During this intense action, Crabbe's tank became disabled and his crew had to abandon it. While continuing to fight on foot he was severely wounded which resulted in his left arm being amputated.

Like much of my work with the wounded during the war, my regimen with him had consisted of monitoring his surgical healing and advising him on physical exercises to help him adjust to civilian life with one arm. He had recently advised me that he was moving to Eagleton Park near Ramsgate. The village had suffered severe damage when a Zeppelin, as part of a group of airships sent to destroy Ramsgate harbour, was forced off course by British fighter pilots. The Germans dropped their ordinance before they crashed, destroying several homes and killing multiple civilians in the area.

After the war, an enterprising Dutch businessman named Jacob Krane had bought up much of the damaged housing, repaired the homes and was offering the first choice of purchase to British former soldiers at substantially reduced prices and interest rates. While the Dutch were officially neutral during the war, Krane recognised that the multiple German violations of that neutrality, such as sinking Dutch ships, would have been even worse had not Britain and her allies intervened. This project was his way of showing gratitude to the brave English soldiers and sailors.

At least this was how Crabbe had explained it to me. He was thrilled that he had been accepted to become one of the new

---

[1] In the Battle of Mericourt and Hangest during World War I, specifically during the Battle of Amiens, the British employed a large number of tanks to attack the German lines along the railway line stretching between these two locations.

residents with his army pension able to meet the relatively low payments. He had no family so moving wasn't an issue.

He had first heard of this project from a fellow wounded veteran, Lieutenant Harvey Masters who had lost a leg in the war. He shared the news with several of his wounded comrades at a club where they gathered. It was one of the few places where they weren't looked upon with pity by the civilian populace.

At one meeting, Masters introduced Krane who spoke of his sympathy for their sacrifice and the gratitude that he was able to express on behalf of the Dutch people. "I have already relocated three other wounded soldiers and Lieutenant Masters will be the fourth after he comes out to inspect the properties tomorrow. There is housing for six more if you qualify."

He passed out applications and advised them. "If you are chosen, you will be invited to view the properties. Upon coming to an agreement on which home you can afford, you will need to put down a minimum deposit of £100 on the spot to reserve it. Of course, the more you can deposit the lower your payments will be. The outright purchase prices range from £450 to £500. We are also offering a below-market interest rate of 2.5% or 3.0% depending on the amount you need to borrow."

Masters had recently moved to Eagleton Park and even sent Crabbe a telegram advising him how wonderful a place it was. Soon Crabbe received news that he had qualified and that he should come down to Ramsgate where Krane would take him out to Eagleton Park to pick out a home to his liking and pay his deposit.

Chapter Two

I was very happy for him. So often our wounded soldiers are forgotten and find themselves in dire straights. The suicide rate among these heroic warriors who sacrificed so much was intolerable because they frequently felt abandoned by their families and their country. This windfall would give him a fair chance at a decent life.

Imagine my surprise then, when four days after he had informed me of his move, ex-Sergeant Crabbe suddenly appeared in my surgery. Haggard and hurting with the growth of three days of beard upon his face, he staggered in and likely would have fallen, had he not the use of a walking stick.

My nurse, recognising his condition, immediately escorted him into my consulting room where he collapsed onto the couch. He did not appear injured, but his breathing was uneven, and his voice hoarse. The nurse quickly brought water while I checked his pulse and temperature. "What's happened to you, Crabbe?" I asked. "Are you injured?"

He shook his head, unable to speak clearly until he took a drink of water. At last, he caught his breath and gasped out a few words, "I've been on the run, Doctor. No time for food or drink. I needed to get to you. I need your friend, Mr. Holmes."

I ordered my nurse to prepare him some broth and bread and tried to keep him calm as he was suffering from shock and some nervous condition. "Holmes lives down in Sussex now. He rarely comes up to London anymore and it will take time

149

for him to get here, even if I can convince him. Tell me, Crabbe, what is it? Why do you need him?"

He took another drink of water, some spilling down his straggly-bearded chin with the effort. Then he looked me in the eye and said, "I've killed a man, Doctor, and I need Holmes to prove that it was self-defence."

Chapter Three

My assistant brought in the food just after he made this statement, so she did not hear it. I helped him to my writing table where he could sit and eat and then dismissed her, telling her that all was under control.

As he spooned the beefy broth into his mouth he spoke between gulps to answer my questions. "Start at the beginning," I said. "Who did you kill?"

"It was Jacob Krane, the lying bastard! And it was him or me! You've got to believe me, Doctor!"

After all my years of working with Holmes, I naturally grabbed pencil and paper and began writing down notes. "Where and when?" I asked.

"Two days ago in Ramsgate, he rasped. Then he shouted, "Supposedly it was Eagleton Park. But there is no Eagleton Park, Dr. Watson. It was all a ruse!"

I tried to calm him down and said, "All right, take your time. Think carefully and give me the details. How did this come about? Weren't you supposed to go down to Eagleton Park with him to examine the homes he had available for disabled soldiers?"

"Yes, all was going as planned. We rode down on the train together and he hired a four-wheeler so that we could drive out to this area where he had supposedly rebuilt homes damaged during the war. We had gone west from the station for about five miles. The houses in that area are spread out with lawns and gardens surrounding each, and there is a small copse of trees that runs along the back of the area.

"He chose to start the tour with the smallest of these houses since I had no family, and so we entered a nice little bungalow. It was freshly painted and quite roomy, having no furniture as yet. The rooms were of good size and well situated to each other.

"He then took me to the back where there was a small outbuilding for a mews and the treeline beyond. I noticed a pile of firewood alongside it This seemed quite convenient, though I didn't know how if I would be able to adapt to chopping wood with one arm. Then I noticed something odd. There was a stick on the stack that was not a branch but rather looked like a finished piece of wood. I stepped closer to get a good look. Just as I realised what it was, I heard a twig on the ground snap behind me. I turned in alarm at what I had seen and now was confronted with its implications. Krane was advancing quickly upon me with an upraised knife!"

"The devil you say!" I exclaimed.

"The devil indeed, Doctor! Fortunately, my military training stood me in good stead. I ducked and rolled under the swipe of his knife and came up behind where I charged him as he turned back to face me and kicked him in the groin. I didn't catch him quite right though, and instead of going down breathless, it merely knocked him off balance and he fell to his knee. I took advantage of this though and quickly wrapped my empty sleeve around his neck. He slashed wildly with his knife, as you will note by the slices on my coat sleeves. But I had a decided advantage. Realising this was going to be a fight to the death I tightened my grip on my chokehold until he breathed no more."

He was breathless from describing the fight so I encouraged him to drink some more water. As he did so I asked him, "What did you see in the woodpile?"

He took a deep breath after a long draught of water and pointed to the walking stick on the floor by the sofa where it had fallen when he sat and replied, "That."

I retrieved it and brought it back to my seat. It was a finely turned oak walking stick with a brass anchor head handle and scrollwork extending from the top around a foot down its length. I noted the initials 'H.L.M.' etched into the handle. "Who is H.L.M.?" I asked.

"Lieutenant Henry Louis Masters," replied the soldier. "I knew it immediately. The Lieutenant used that to help steady him on his artificial leg. He would never part with it. Krane must have thrown it onto the wood pile to be burned but didn't get around to it before he brought me along. He must have recognised his error by my reaction and that's why he attacked me when he did."

I pondered what my patient was telling me as he ate some more broth, dipping the bread into it. Finally, I leaned back to be less intimidating and recounted what he had said.

"So, it is your contention that Krane was running this scheme to get disabled soldiers to invest in a fake property, steal their deposit money, kill them, and then repeat the whole thing with someone new."

He swallowed a mouthful of broth and replied, "That's all I can figure, Doctor. He probably sent the telegram in Masters's name himself to make me think all was as advertised. He might well have only the one property instead of the several he claimed. He could show it over and over again, and easily overpower the disabled clients and pocket their money."

I nodded, "What did you do with Krane's body?"

"I dragged it to the mews. There was a bag of quicklime in there so I shovelled some over him to hide the smell, then covered him with a tarpaulin and closed the door."

"Why not go to the police and tell them your story?"

Crabbe dabbed his mouth with a napkin and leaned forward to keep our conversation as quiet as possible, even though the door between us and my nurse was closed. He rubbed the growth of beard on his jaw and finally said, "I've been in trouble with the law before, Dr. Watson. Assault and battery during a bar fight three years ago. Put a fellow into the hospital, but I didn't kill him, I swear! Just laid him up for a while. The judge was not convinced that the witnesses were

153

telling the truth about who started the fight, but he couldn't very well let me go. I got sentenced to three years.

"Anyway that's on my record and I didn't want some police officer using my past against me to try and make this into a murder case instead of the self-defence that it is. I knew Mr. Holmes would come at it with an unprejudiced eye. That's why I left Ramsgate and came to find you in as roundabout a manner as I could in case the body was discovered."

Chapter Four

I certainly sympathised with Crabbe and had no reason to doubt his story. As it was late afternoon and I had no more patients to see for the day, I decided that the safest course of action would be to let him stay in my spare room until I could convince Holmes to come up to town.

Fortunately, Crabbe and I were roughly the same size so I provided him with a fresh change of clothes after he had taken a bath and had a shave. While he was doing that, I got on the telephone and called Holmes.

As these were the days of party lines when strangers could listen in on phone calls, I used an old code which Holmes and I had developed while working on the Millais forgery case[1] several years before.

Our conversation went something to the effect of:

"Holmes? Watson here."

"Watson, dear chap. How are you?"

"Oh, the usual. Just some issues with Doyle."

"I am sorry to hear that. Anything you need from me?"

"No, I can handle him. But I have been invited to partake in a golf tournament and need a partner. Are you up for a match?"

"I could come up for a couple of days. Will tomorrow be convenient?"

---

[1] *Sketches of a Blackmailer* in *The Colourful Cases of Sherlock Holmes, Vol 2* published by Baker Street Studios Limited in 2024.

"That will be ideal. Could you contact Lestrade to see if he would like to join us? Don't worry about a hotel, I can put you both up here."

"Splendid! I should arrive on the late morning train."

"Excellent. I shall see you then. *Au revoir*."

Of course, to anyone listening, it all sounded innocent enough. But my use of the name Doyle meant that I had a case for him. The reference to golf indicated it was for a client and not myself, and the invitation to stay with me advised him that we would be traveling elsewhere. Including Lestrade meant that he should bring his Bassett hound named after the Scotland Yard Inspector. *Au revoir* was code for him to bring his revolver, just in case.

At ten minutes past ten o'clock the next morning, Holmes arrived at my door, carpetbag in one hand and golf bag slung over his other shoulder with Lestrade on his leash. I welcomed him heartily and invited him into my parlour where I introduced him to Crabbe. Lestrade waddled over to the ex-soldier, sniffed him and, then nuzzled his hand.

"Well that certainly counts in your favour, Crabbe," said Holmes, offering his own hand in greeting. "Lestrade is an excellent judge of character."

I had advised my assistant at the end of the previous day that she could have the next three days off so we were quite alone to discuss matters and make our plans. I put down a water bowl for the hound and the three of us took up chairs around my fireplace to give the detective the details of Crabbe's case.

When Crabbe had finished his story, Holmes pursed his lips and slowly nodded, "I understand your reluctance to contact the police. They are often too quick to judge, but are you absolutely sure that Krane did not have an accomplice? No one who might come looking for him?"

Crabbe tilted his head, "The thought never occurred to me, Mr. Holmes. Krane came alone to all our meetings and he made no mention of anyone else. I don't recall him ever using the word 'we'."

Holmes replied, "I only mention it as it is unlikely that he made the repairs to the house himself, even if you are correct and it was only the single property. Did you ever happen to notice if his hands were calloused from manual labour?"

Crabbe thought back, "Well, I shook his hand on at least two occasions and they were more the hands of a clerk, though I did notice a blister under his right little finger."

"Possibly he did the repairs himself or merely paid an unassociated contractor to do so. The blister may have been from digging graves to bury his victims. Did you notice any disturbed earth in the area?"

"There may have been some beyond the mews among the trees, Mr. Holmes, but I never got that far before I saw Masters's cane."

"Well, we shall venture out to Ramsgate in the morning and see what evidence we can gather to prove your innocence."

Chapter Five

We caught an early train and were in Ramsgate by 10.45 the next morning. The smell of the sea was strong in the air, even though we were over a mile inland from the harbour. Holmes had provided Crabbe with a disguise for his face and a cloak to hide his missing arm. We rented a gig and the soldier guided us to the location of the incident.

We pulled around to the mews in the back so as not to draw attention to ourselves. Before disembarking, Holmes asked Crabbe to point out where the various stages of the fight with Krane had happened.

He indicated a spot about halfway between the house and the mews, "We were just there. Krane was about a pace behind me as he was describing the boundaries of the property. That's where we were when I spotted Masters's cane."

"How is it that you were able to identify it at a glance?" asked Holmes.

Crabbe hung his head in sorrow. "I feel that I am to blame for his injury, Mr Holmes. When I was wounded after we were forced to abandon our tank, it was the Lieutenant who rushed to my aid to assist me to safety. It was as he helped me towards cover under a barrage of German gunfire that he received the wounds that cost him his leg. I have tried to help him however I could through his ordeal. That cane belonged to my grandfather, a naval captain. I thought it fitting that it should go to another officer and so it was I who gave it to Masters."

I commented, "Your loyalty does you credit, sir."

He merely nodded, "It was the least I could do, Doctor. I am only sorry for his senseless end at the hands of this charlatan, Krane. I cannot say that I am sorry for what I did to him for it was as much out of vengeance as it was self-defence."

Holmes spoke up, "I suggest that you keep that part to yourself when you talk to the police, Crabbe. Self-defence should be quite sufficient. There's no use confusing them with a secondary motive which could affect the measure of your guilt in their eyes. Wait here while I examine the grounds."

Carefully Holmes, with Lestrade on his leash, circled the area where the confrontation had occurred. He approached cautiously, so as not to disturb the existing tracks and any traces. He made a minute examination of the lawn, mumbling to himself and taking measurements. Encouraging the hound to sniff the area where the body had fallen, he then followed the drag marks to the mews. Upon opening the door he turned and called, "You may now join me gentlemen, but mind your step."

Once inside we left the door open to have daylight by which to see. Holmes drew back the tarpaulin to reveal the body of Jacob Krane. The quicklime had done its work in minimising the smell of decomposition. Holmes performed a cursory examination but more specifically concentrated on Krane's boots to ensure that they matched the tracks he had found outside. He asked me to verify the cause of death, and when I examined the victim's neck the ligature marks from Crabbe's sleeve were obvious. The pressure applied dislocated the vertebrae at position C5 and appeared to have fractured the hyoid bone.

While I was doing this, Lestrade was sniffing the area and Holmes was checking the ground. We soon saw him open the back door and follow the hound out and into the woods. When I asked him where he was going he called back, "Please remain where you are. I'll be back momentarily."

True to his word he was back in around three minutes. "Crabbe," he said, "I see that Krane's knife is next to his body, I presume that you picked it up and placed it there?"

"Yes, Mr. Holmes, but I took it by the blade. I didn't want my fingerprints anywhere near the handle, just so I could prove it was him that drew it on me."

Holmes smiled, "A wise precaution. Doctor, you may cover him back up. I believe, gentlemen, that we may now report this matter to the police with every confidence in our case for self-defence."

We drove towards the harbour. Having worked here before, Holmes recalled the location of the police station. We arrived just before one o'clock, and upon Holmes presenting his card at the front desk he advised the officer on desk duty that he wished to report a crime to the highest-ranking officer present. At that moment the officer sought walked through the door, having returned from lunch. It transpired to be Assistant Chief Constable Matthew Pritchard who welcomed us and bid us to follow him to his office.

There was a sofa to one side and Holmes indicated that Crabbe should sit there with Lestrade at his feet while he and I took up the guest chairs opposite Pritchard's desk. Once settled the official asked us what we had to report.

"My client, ex-Sergeant Thomas Crabbe, wishes to turn himself in for an official investigation to find a verdict of self-defence in the death of one Jacob Krane, who attempted to kill him, and has apparently killed four other men prior to Crabbe putting an end to his spree."

Pritchard, a middle-aged, clean-shaven man with a strongly built stature, square jaw and penetrating blue eyes, leaned back in his chair to digest this revelation. He gave away no emotion of surprise or dismay but took in the information dispassionately and professionally.

After a moment to consider, Pritchard leaned forward, folding his hands upon his desktop and stared at our client. "Mr. Crabbe, I must advise you that anything you say can be used against you. Do you concur that this is the action you wish to take and that you are confessing to the killing of this man Krane, or do you wish to remain silent?"

Crabbe sat up straight and met the Assistant Chief Constable's eyes with a steady gaze of his own. "I killed him, sir. But it was self-defence and that's why I went to Mr. Holmes so that he could prove it."

Pritchard frowned, then took up a pencil and paper, "Just where and when did this incident occur?"

"Eagleton Park, four days ago."

Pritchard squinted at him and, with a trace of anger remonstrated him, "Four days ago! Why did you wait so long if it was self-defence? And where in blazes is Eagleton Park?"

Holmes stepped in at this point, "If you will allow me, Mr. Pritchard, in the course of your investigation you will find that Mr. Crabbe has a previous arrest. He wished to lay out his story to a neutral third party before coming to the official police. As I now live in Sussex it took some time for us to connect, but I have now examined the scene of the crime for myself and concur that it was self-defence. I shall be happy to lend my assistance to your investigation to prove these facts to you. As to Eagleton Park, that name itself was made up by Mr. Krane and is one of the proofs that he was a dishonest man."

Pritchard tapped the pencil in a quick staccato burst upon his desk and finally said, "I don't like it, Mr. Holmes. If it were anyone other than you I'd hold you for obstruction of justice. This isn't 1895 anymore and we are not the overworked inspectors of old Scotland Yard. The rules are more restrictive these days. But as it is let's get all the facts and see where we go from here."

Crabbe told his story from the beginning with Krane's offer of low-cost housing to disabled ex-soldiers, to his discovery of Masters's cane and the attack by Krane. He was a little vague on the timeline as to his getting to me, and me getting to Holmes, and Holmes travelling to London, but all in all, it was accurate to what we had been told.

When finished, Pritchard invited Crabbe to review his notes and sign them until an official statement could be typed up. Then he said, "Very well since we have a good deal of daylight left, let's go and see this crime scene and determine the facts. As we left the police station Pritchard called out, "Sergeant Ruxton, come with us!"

A burly fellow with a uniform bulging with muscles and a thick blond moustache grabbed his coat and followed. He drove the Assistant Chief Constable behind our four-wheeler and we led the way to the crime scene. Upon arrival, when all had disembarked, Pritchard looked at Holmes and said, "This Krane fellow claimed that this was Eagleton Park?"

"Yes, the London Disabled Soldiers Club will be able to verify that for you."

"This is still the suburb of Newington. There was some bomb damage done here during the war but that has all been repaired. I know of no foreigners being involved."

Crabbe piped up, "I think Krane bought this place and lied about everything else."

"Well, we'll see," replied Pritchard non-committally. "So, Mr. Holmes, show me your evidence."

Holmes led the way to the area of the lawn showing the footmarks where the struggle had taken place. He explained how the prints of Crabbe's boots were different from Krane's and demonstrated how Crabbe had been able to use his army training to get the upper hand and get Krane into the chokehold that killed him.

"We also have this evidence," added the detective moving closer to the mews doorway. "Note that we again have the prints of Mr. Krane. But see these prints here?"

Pritchard looked but shook his head. "I only see another bootprint that could just as easily be Kranes."

Holmes knelt and pointed, "We have been fortunate in that the weather has been so mild as of late. These marks are those which correspond to *those* bootprints," he indicated. "Which are a full two sizes larger than Kranes."

"What are those holes in the ground?"

"They were produced by Lieutenant Masters's peg leg. See by the pattern that it was here where Krane stabbed Masters who fell against the door, note the scratches sliding downwards, likely caused by his sleeve buttons as he tried to keep himself upright.

"From here Krane threw Masters's walking stick onto the woodpile, and dragged the body inside from where he loaded it in a wheelbarrow and took it off for burial."

We followed the drag marks into the mews and uncovered the body of Krane for Pritchard to examine.

After his inspection, Pritchard rose and said, "Well it checks out so far. But how do you know that he killed Masters and the others?"

Holmes crooked his finger and, letting Lestrade lead the way, he pointed to the ground as we made our way out the back door and towards the woods, "See here the tracks of a wheelbarrow, and every so often some bits of quicklime have fallen as it was transported. The footprints following it are a match to Krane's boots."

Finally, Lestrade came to a halt. We looked around but saw nothing. Pritchard asked the obvious, "Why are we here, Mr. Holmes?"

In reply, Holmes bent down, threw back a patch of weeds revealing a hole in a wooden sheet and lifted it. In this uplifted position it now exposed a large crater, roughly six feet square and perhaps eight feet deep. Piled roughly in the bottom were the bodies of four men, covered in quicklime and in varying stages of decay. All were in uniform. The previous clients of Jacob Krane.

Pritchard turned away, sickened by the sight. Ruxton braved a closer look, then turned up his nose and walked away shaking his head. Crabbe fell to his knees at the side of the hole, having recognised his friend, Masters, and began to weep. Holmes let the wooden sheet fall back over the mass grave and recovered the handhold with the weed patch again to keep others from finding it before the police could recover the bodies.

When our nerves had settled Pritchard turned to my friend and said, "You have made your case, Mr. Holmes. I will still have to follow protocol and hold your client until we finish the post mortem and can verify his story, but I believe that will all be a formality and that no official charges will appear against him."

Turning to Crabbe he said, "Please be kind enough to go with Sergeant Ruxton back to our car. The law says that I must hold you, but under the circumstances, we will try to make your stay with us as comfortable as possible. With any luck, we should have all this settled in a very few days and then I will be able to send you on your way."

As the two men left us, Pritchard turned to the detective, "Mr. Holmes, I never thought I'd have the pleasure of meeting you, but I am right glad that you came out of retirement for this case and assured that we found all the evidence to keep an honourable ex-soldier from being prosecuted. Thank you, sir."

He shook Holmes's hand and we accompanied him back to the vehicles. Assuring Crabbe that we would stay in touch until the case was complete, we left him in Pritchard's hands while we returned to the railway station and caught the evening train back to London. Holmes stayed with me for the few days until Crabbe's case was dismissed, during which we spent the time reminiscing over old cases. He gave me some further details of an adventure that I have since published under the title of *His Last Bow.*

He did make one comment regarding my writings, however, when he stated this to me:

"Should you choose to publish this case, Watson, you will naturally change the names of those involved to avoid any future repercussions. May I suggest something along the lines of Crab and Crane? The case is very similar to the old Indian Panchatantra tale of that name.[1]"

As the reader will note, I have followed Holmes's advice, as it is usually the wisest thing to do.

---

[1] The Panchatantra Tales were ancient animal stories by Vishnu Sharma written for children to learn moral lessons; very much like Aesop's Fables of Ancient Greece. The story of the crab and the crane is one in which a crane lies to a colony of crabs and offers to take them to a wonderful new home, but actually stops and eats each one that he fools along the way.

Leo: The Lion
(23rd July – 22nd August)

The Lioness in Winter

Confident but dominating. Born to be under the spotlight, there is nothing that this lion enjoys as much as being the centre of attention However, this conviction that they are always in the right means that they can often run roughshod over the feelings and sentiments of others.

Chapter One

Leona Pride was the toast of theatrical circles since her debut in 1880 in *The Pirates of Penzance*. Over the years her fame grew and she became known as the 'Regina Diva', of the London stage. I, myself, had seen her in multiple productions over the years, in roles that varied from Shakespeare to Irving, Stoker, Yeats, Shaw, Wilde and Gilbert & Sullivan. I had also heard the whispers of her more derogatory reputation as 'The Lioness of the West End'. She was demanding, arrogant and egotistical. Her talent allowed this unfortunate personality to develop because every producer wanted her and was willing to pander to her demands. There was never a season in which she did not perform as a leading lady in a major theatrical production. There was a failed marriage when she was in her twenties and she never came to the altar again, nor had she any children.

Her career spanned over three decades and it was at the end of that professional life which brought about a case for my long-time friend, the detective, Sherlock Holmes. He had recently returned to England, having spent some time in the United States of America on a government assignment which I would only learn the details of a year later[1]. In point of fact, he

---

[1] Sir Arthur Conan Doyle would give more details of this assignment in his short story *His Last Bow. The War Service of Sherlock Holmes* which was published in *The Strand Magazine* in 1917.

was still on that assignment, though now on British soil in the guise of a disgruntled Irishman. However, a special commission from Queen Mary brought him back to London. He could not return to Baker Street, nor could he stay at the Diogenes Club without exciting comment on his presence. Therefore, to remain incognito, he stayed with me and my wife.

He had not told me the details of the Queen's request when he contacted me. He only asked if he could come up for a discreet visit. I certainly had no need of an explanation, for I could never refuse him as he always had excellent reasons for his actions. He arrived on Wednesday 22nd September after dark, but before dinner. As I was expecting him, I took it upon myself to answer the door. Before me, stood a bowed, lean, old clergyman with a hooked nose, grey hair escaping from beneath his broad-brimmed hat and mutton-chop sideboards of a nearly white shade. His clerical collar stood out against his black suit and his right arm shook as he leaned on his cane. Recognising this as one of his old disguises, I merely greeted him with a warm "Welcome, Reverend. Please do come in."

I assured him that we had given our servant-girl a few days off and that only my wife and I were at home. She had stood back in the doorway to the dining room while I had answered the door, but now strode forward.

"Good evening, *Reverend*" she said, extending her hand, which he took and bowed over politely as I closed the door behind him. "You have just time refresh yourself before dinner, or do you plan on remaining in disguise?"

He had straightened to his full height and replied, "I should enjoy one of your superbly cooked meals, my dear. However, I do have to go out again later and must maintain my masquerade for that task."

"Very well," she replied. "John can show you to your room and by the time you have freshened up I will have dinner on the table."

Chapter Two

In five minutes Holmes and I had returned to the dining room and my wife was laying out the last of the serving dishes. I had attempted to learn why Holmes had come to town, but he put me off suggesting that he did not wish to deprive my wife of the story.

Once we had settled into our chairs and said grace, we started passing around the food and I encouraged my friend to tell us all. As he sliced up his food into bite-sized pieces he told us the task which had been set before him.

"You have no doubt read of the death of Leona Pride, the actress?" he began.

My wife responded, "Yes, it is such a shame so great a talent was lost to us so young."

Holmes smiled, "It is amazing what proper makeup can do. She was not so young as you think. I imagine it would surprise you to learn that she was fifty-five years old."

I was startled by this revelation, "How can that be, Holmes? She began her career when she was a mere seventeen."

The detective shook his head, "Like many actresses, she lied about her age to appear suitable to that first part as one of the Major-General's daughters in the original production of the *Pirates of Penzance*. She was actually twenty-three but has continued to use her fake birth year of 1863. She was really born in 1858 under the name Leonora Rippetoe. She shortened Leonora to Leona which translates roughly to lioness. That led her to choose Pride as a more suitable surname for a marquee with a linguistic link to the lion species."

I shook my head in astonishment, then inquired, "So you are here to investigate her death? Why has Queen Mary taken such an interest that she would request you specifically?"

Holmes steepled his fingers and took on that tone he uses when imparting information that is only peripheral to a case. "When the Queen was a child, her mother, the Duchess of Teck, used to involve her quite often in her various charities and these included visiting the homes of the poor. Apparently, this is where she met Leonora and struck up a friendship of sorts as they were only a year apart in age. She followed Leonora's career and they exchanged letters, even when the Princess was living overseas later on.

"Leona's death has some suspicious aspects to it which Scotland Yard has not been able to resolve. The fact that it took place on the night of her final performance is too convenient to be coincidental. There is concern that someone may have decided to end her career to make way for someone else."

My wife spoke up, "There was nothing in the papers about murder. She was reported to have had a heart attack."

Holmes nodded, "The Yard has kept the details quiet. She did, in truth, die of a heart attack. But what has not been reported is the fact that it was brought on by poison."

Chapter Three

That hat statement took my wife and I aback into shocked silence for a moment. When I recovered my wits I said, "So you are here to solve a murder?"

Holmes amended my remark, "I am here to discover the truth, whichever direction it takes and to whomever it might lead."

He took his last bite of food and followed it with a sip of wine, then changed the subject as if he had no more to say about his mission. "I must tell you, Doctor, that your leaving Baker Street for this inestimable bride of yours, severely reduced the quality of Mrs. Hudson's cooking."

Despite this abrupt shift in conversation, my wife, with that great capacity she has for caring for others, asked with concern in her voice, "Is she all right?"

Holmes nodded and reassured us, "Other than some minor pains of her age, she is quite healthy. No, I am merely convinced that your husband was her favourite tenant and that after he left us for married bliss with you, I was only getting the dregs of her cuisine."

I laughed, "Considering how your diary rarely coincided with her food preparation when you were on a case, I am not surprised that she reduced her cooking routine to a minimum. How many times over the years did you actually thank her for a meal?"

He straightened up and I could see his brain start searching for a calculation. I shook my head, "If you have to think about it, Holmes, it wasn't often enough."

He frowned, then said, "Well, I shall have to be more cognizant of offering my gratitude." Turning back to my wife he said in his most gracious tone, "Starting now. My dear, your cooking is most excellent and this is the finest meal I've had in months. Thank you."

"You are quite welcome, Sherlock. As long as you keep your promise to bring John safely home to me from these little adventures of yours, you shall always be welcome at this table. Now what steps will you be taking and how can we help?"

That was always the case with my wife. Not content with the routine of the mistress of the house now that her children were grown and gone, she was always looking for ways to assist others. She was deeply involved in charity work, but an adventuress streak in her craves an occasional rush of excitement.

Holmes gave her a long look and responded, "I am still considering the best path of investigation. However, one of the options may require the need of a female presence, if the Doctor doesn't mind."

I looked to my wife and smiled, "As if I could stop her! Anything either of us can do to help is always available to you, Holmes. So long as you keep the same promise to me, to bring her home safely."

"I foresee no danger. If there was indeed a murder, it was methodical and well-planned. Not a crime of passion which would make the killer less predictable and harder to defend against. If I pursue this option, her role would be to blend in and gather information surreptitiously.

"However," he said as he stood, "I must first examine the scene, get the lay of the land and gather what information I can from the authorities. The difficulty will be in keeping my name out of it. I will have to take someone at Scotland Yard into my confidence and I am debating between Lestrade and Hopkins. I will also need to see the police surgeon's findings and the coroner's report."

I spoke up, "I can deal with Dr. Fox and the coroner's office, Holmes. My relationships with them can get me access with a suitable excuse without bringing your name into it. I can tell them that since your retirement I am looking to expand my writing and am exploring the possibility of doing Miss Pride's biography."

Holmes bowed in gratitude, "Thank you, Doctor. I shall start then with the theatre. She was found in her dressing room and the manager there is an old friend whom I can trust completely. I should be able to take care of that tonight now that the theatre is dark while in rehearsals for the next production. I will be gone for no more than three hours. When I return we can make our battle plans."

After he had left, my wife and I retired to the parlour with some wine and sat before the warm fire. She asked me if I had any ideas as to who might wish to kill Leona Pride.

I smiled as I recalled another case, "Very early in our association, in fact, I believe it was our first year at Baker Street, we had a case regarding an actor being threatened.[1] During that affair Holmes recited a list of motives that were specifically related to the theatrical profession."

"Really? How could he do that?" asked my wife.

"He compared it to a doctor narrowing his diagnosis depending on the symptoms. I believe among actors the primary motives for murder were envy, jealousy, frustration and hatred. Of course, he never completely ruled out other possibilities such as fear or revenge. But, he starts his hypotheses with those specific ideas in mind. So, I would imagine that he would look for a poisoner with the necessary skills and access to commit the crime along with one of those motives."

She nodded and replied, "He will probably concentrate on other actresses then. Hasn't he said that poison is usually a woman's weapon of choice? An actress who was bitter over Leona's always getting the leading role and blocking the career path of others would be the most likely suspect in my mind."

---

[1] *The Neopolitan Complexity* by Roger Riccard published in *The Colourful Cases of Sherlock Holmes, Volume 3* by Baker Street Studios Limited in 2024.

Chapter Four

Holmes's evening was informative, though not conclusive. Leona Pride had been performing as Lady Anne in *Richard III*. The theatre had sealed off her dressing room, which was the scene of her death, by order of Scotland Yard. In his clergyman disguise, Holmes confided his true identity to the stage manager and had him agree to the concocted story that as 'Reverend Shubert' he was there to collect such things as may be conducive to Miss Pride's memorial service and burial. This was only in the event that someone should happen to see him there, although the timing of Holmes's visit had coincided with the rehearsals for the next production and, as those took place during the day, it was unlikely that anyone should be about. He asked the manager about Pride's understudy and was informed that she had none. "She was too proud to allow it," he said. "She insisted that if she became ill or injured, the performances be halted until she returned."

Holmes moved on to the dressing room and began a systematic search for anything unusual. The police had collected items which might have contained poison, so he would have to depend on Dr. Fox's reports on that account. For now, he was seeking evidence of either murder or suicide. On one wall were tacked reviews of her current performance, all of which seemed favourable.

There was also a newspaper clipping regarding the recent motion picture of *Hamlet*. Reviewers who had been allowed a private screening prior to its release were hailing it as a *tour de force* in the art of entertainment. A paragraph praising Gertrude Elliot as Ophelia was underlined and a handwritten note in the margin stated 'this should be me!'.

A detailed search showed that Scotland Yard had been efficient in its collection of evidence. A sign to him that it was likely Inspector Stanley Hopkins in charge. Holmes considered Hopkins a protégé of sorts since they met back in the nineties and Hopkins, unlike those at the Yard who resented the consulting detective, was always eager to learn and emulate Holmes's methods.

He did find one particular item that he felt may be relevant and stuffed it into the inner pocket of his overcoat along with the newspaper clipping before he left. He asked the stage manager the home address of the deceased and whether she had any servants. He was informed that she had a valet who also acted as her driver, a housekeeper/cook and a maidservant/dresser. Bidding the gentleman good evening he stepped out into the alley behind the theatre. It was there that he noticed a series of rubbish bins at which point another thought occurred to him. However, it would be unseemly for his clergyman persona to dig around the waste. He walked to the main road and found what, or rather who, he needed. Two of his old Baker Street Irregulars were playing on harmonicas before a container on the pavement, collecting alms for their performance. He called them over and promised a shilling apiece to search the theatre's bins for a specific item.

They were eager to earn such a sum and immediately began rummaging through the receptacles. Between them, they found five of the kind of items Holmes was seeking. Pleased by their diligence and success, he gave them an extra shilling each and swore them to secrecy regarding his presence in London.

He returned to our home just after nine o'clock and joined my wife and I for a nightcap whereupon made a request to use my medical instruments and chemicals to conduct some experiments on what he had found.

As we sat with libations in hand, my wife asked, "Do you believe that you have discovered evidence of foul play?"

Holmes gave that enigmatic smile of his, which I often found to be irritating when he was holding something back, and replied, "Depending upon the results of my experiments and tomorrow's interviews I should be able to determine the truth of the matter. I can tell you that I believe there is something at play here, but as to its foulness, I cannot be certain as yet."

While we retired for the evening, Holmes ensconced himself in my medical suite and began his experiments. I do not know when he finished for he was gone when we arose in the morning. All he left was a note saying that he was off to see Inspector Hopkins and would return to pick me up to interview Miss Pride's servants and expected that we would be home for lunch after that. I noticed the containers which he had swabbed for chemical residue. Based on their labels, none seemed to have comprised anything lethal and I wondered what he was thinking.

I took the opportunity to visit Dr. Fox and see what the police surgeon had found. There were definitely traces of poison in her system. "It was inhaled, Dr. Watson. But I cannot be definitive as to whether it was fumes from her makeup, the spray she used for her throat, or her snuff. The chemical analyses of those items have not been completed yet, but I will let you know when they are. However, I can tell you, that even without the poison, she would have been dead in a matter of months from throat cancer."

This was something Holmes needed to hear. I thanked Fox for his assistance and returned home to await my friend. It was not long in coming and he wasted no time but kept the cab waiting while he fetched me. *En route* to Miss Pride's home, he filled me in on his visit to Scotland Yard. "Hopkins has been quite thorough. He allowed me to see all the various items collected from Miss Pride's dressing room … the combination paints a dire picture."

I looked at my friend with concern, "Dr. Fox agrees that her death was not natural, but he has yet to determine how the poison was administered. However, it would have been a natural death in a matter of months, possibly weeks. She was dying of throat cancer. But someone decided to hurry the process along.

"Fox says it was advanced and that the chemicals found among her makeup and dressing room items indicated that she was self-medicating in order to be able to say her lines on stage loud enough. Had it gone on much longer the dosage required would have put her into a mental state that would have hampered her performance. Her career was coming to an end and her life would soon follow."

As Holmes pondered that for a moment, I added, "Could her self-medicating have resulted in an accidental overdose, or perhaps she was suicidal?"

He folded his long fingers into his lap and answered, "That is what we must ascertain. I did discover that she was an addicted consumer of snuff. As you are aware that is not something well-bred ladies indulge in publicly, though it was known to be a favourite habit of Queen Charlotte[1] a century ago. I believe Fox will find that her snuff box contained pure cocaine mixed in with the fine tobacco and I found a container in the rubbish with trace amounts of cocaine. How the two came together is something we must determine. I trust that our conversation with her servants will give us more data regarding her moods and any enemies that she may have had."

We soon arrived at one of the smaller properties in Chelsea where Leona Pride lived in a suite of rooms on the top floor of a red brick and white-columned building typical to the area built during the reigns of the Georgian Kings.

We crunched through a layer of red and yellow leaves covering the pavement. As we were expected, the valet, Hawkins by name, immediately opened the door, showed us in, took our coats and brought us to the sitting room where glimpses of the Thames could be seen to the south. Holmes had removed his clerical collar and straightened to his full height upon our arrival, but retained the rest of his disguise and

---

[1] George III's Queen Charlotte was so fond of snuff that she earned the nickname 'Snuffy Charlotte'.

presented himself as 'Inspector Shubert', whereas I was still Dr. John Watson.

"To whom would you wish to speak first, Inspector?" Hawkins asked. The man was young, handsome, tall and clean-shaven. I would have put his age at no more than thirty, but he comported himself in the fashion of an experienced servant. Holmes replied that he wanted to start with the maidservant so Hawkins went to fetch Miss Flora Stanton.

The young lady he brought back appeared to be in her late teens. Brown curls escaped from under her mop cap and framed her cherubic face. She was a little plump but well-fitted into her maid's uniform. She looked after Hawkins as he left the room and due to her youth, I expected her to be nervous, but she sat up straight and her expression was one of confidence. She answered Holmes's questions calmly and without hesitation. Her primary concern was what her future held now that her mistress was gone.

Holmes's questioning covered a variety of topics. Regarding health, Miss Stanton declared that the actress was having frequent sore throats and had taken to writing down her instructions for the day. She also seemed to be spending considerable time at her typewriter, an unusual instrument to be found in a private home, especially that of an actress. The maid said that it was a recent addition, only having arrived four months ago.

"We have come to find that Miss Pride was a user of snuff," said Holmes. "Would you say it was obsessively constant, or perhaps just once or twice per day?"

"I knew she had it, Inspector, for the container was in her bedroom and I've seen her snuff box. But I never actually saw her use it, so I would think it was infrequent."

"Was the box out in the open where anyone could have access to it?"

"Well, yes, Inspector Shubert. But there would be no reason for anyone to touch it, except perhaps to clean around it since it was on her dresser next to her jewellery box."

Changing subjects Holmes asked about possible enemies. She knew of none but was aware of a growing resentment by her mistress of a man named Hepworth. She did not know who he was or indeed Miss Pride's issue with him. Only that she would occasionally be reading a newspaper or magazine and suddenly throw it down while spitting out his name in a vicious invective.

When asked about any close friends of the actress she replied, "Her social engagements have declined in recent months and she rarely visited any particular individuals. She was mostly attracted to events with large gatherings of people where she could be seen and admired."

Thinking of her beauty, even now in her fifties, I asked about her escorts, "Did she have any particular male companions taking her to these events? A love interest, perhaps?"

Holmes nodded his approval at my question and leaned forward keenly for the answer. This was where Miss Stanton gave her only moment of hesitation. She drew back deeper into her chair while she thought about her reply. Finally, with a look towards the door to ensure that it was closed, she leaned forward and said, "Will you promise not to reveal it was I who told you this?"

I looked to Holmes and he tilted his head in curiosity, then said, "Unless you are about to reveal something illegal, we shall be discreet in your regard. What do you have to tell us?"

In a whisper, with her elbows on her knees as she leaned closer, she responded, "Miss Pride's preference was to go to these events alone to see what men she might attract." She took a hard swallow and then, continued, "On more than one occasion she did not return until the following morning and was not always sober. The state of her dress indicated that she had removed it at some point and was unsuccessful in reattaching all the buttons when putting it back on."

The young lady buried her face in her hands for a moment while we digested the meaning behind her observation. Then she looked up again. "There's more ..."

But she did not continue her statement for several moments, leaving us to our imaginations. What secrets had she still to tell? Could her tale give us insight into a murderer? At last, she spoke again and I had to strain to hear her whisper. "Last summer she just stopped going to social outings. Her excuse was always the heat, or that she was too tired from rehearsals or performances. But I believe that it was her health because that was about the time the sore throats started. But her ... physical appetite did not stop. I have seen and heard enough to know that Mr. Hawkins became her ... I believe the term is *gigolo*?"

I gaped at this pronouncement but Holmes merely nodded and said quietly, "It is not uncommon among wealthy women, though certainly more usual for older men to keep a young mistress. Does Hawkins know that you are aware of this relationship?"

She shook her head, "We have never spoken of it, sir. Which is why I ask you to keep my secret. I don't know what he might do to me for spilling the goods."

"Does the housekeeper know?"

"I don't know, Inspector. I certainly didn't tell her. I didn't want to get sacked for spreading gossip, even if it was true."

"Very well. We shall find out without mentioning your knowledge of the fact. Holmes thought for a moment then asked, "Where is this typewriter that you say she began using?"

"On the writing desk in her bedroom, sir. She was very private about it and didn't want it in the parlour where someone might accidentally see what she was typing."

"Very well. That is all for now. Please tell Hawkins to send in the housekeeper."

While we waited, I said to my companion, "Holmes, why would Leona Pride risk her career and reputation consorting with multiple men? And how could she take on a lover young enough to be her son?"

He shook his head, "Think of her personality, Watson. She was fierce and demanding, not the ideal lady any man would want to settle down with for a marriage. Yet her appetites needed to be sated. As her illness worsened, she could not risk it becoming known to the outside world. Mr. Hawkins is handsome and likely vigorous to meet her needs. She was still a beautiful woman so their age difference would be no matter to him. And she knew, that he, being in her pay, would keep any health issue she had a secret because his income depended upon her career success."

"It's indecent!" I argued.

Holme shrugged his shoulders and said, "I leave all matters of love to you, dear Doctor. But unless it figures into a crime of murder, I have no reason to judge their relationship."

Before I could respond further the door opened and Hawkins ushered in the housekeeper who was also the cook. She was a widow named Mrs. Carlotti. I put her age in her mid-forties, as streaks of grey were just beginning to interrupt the waves of raven hair tied into a ponytail behind her back. Her olive skin and facial features confirmed the Italian heritage indicated by her name. She spoke excellent English however, with no trace of an accent. She sat down in the chair Holmes indicated with her hands folded neatly in her lap. Her walnut brown eyes darted between us in nervousness and before Holmes could begin, she asked a question of her own. "I beg your pardon, sir, but do you know what is to become of us now that our mistress is no longer here to serve?"

I noticed a slight speech impediment as she spoke, and could see that she had a few teeth protruding in errant directions. I wondered if this caused her concern about finding a new position, either way it certainly removed her from any suspicion on my part. Holmes advised her that we were not aware of what their future held, and that it would be up to whomever Miss Pride had designated in her will.

She looked downcast in resignation then simply nodded before saying, "What do you wish to ask of me?"

Holmes directed her through his usual list of questions and then added a new one based on the information that we had obtained. "It is rumoured that your mistress recently took up a new lover. Do you know who that was and whether he might have some reason to wish her harm to gain some advantage over her estate?"

She was taken aback by the frankness of my friend's question. Putting a hand to her breast she leaned backwards as if to put some distance between herself and the unpleasant fact that we had brought into the open. Finally, she took a deep breath and with resolve spoke, "Sir, I will not speak of such things. My mistress's personal life was private and no one else's business. I know of no lover who would wish her harm in this matter. There were some letters that I saw her reading which seemed to upset her, but I do not know who they were from."

Holmes's interest was piqued, "Do you know where these letters are?"

"I do not know if she kept them, they seemed to anger her so. If she did, I imagine that they would be in the writing desk in her room."

I thought to myself, these letters would not have come from Hawkins since he lived in the house. Perhaps there was an unknown enemy and Queen Mary was right to be concerned.

Chapter Five

Holmes dismissed the woman and that left us with Hawkins to interview. Holmes bade him to sit down and relax, however true to his station Hawkins maintained a bolt-upright posture in his chair. His square jaw was set like granite and his steely blue eyes were as sharp as flint.

Rather than questioning the man as he had the ladies, Holmes chose a different tactic. "Mr. Hawkins, I do not wish to interrogate you with endless questions. Let me instead, advise you as to what we have been told by your fellow servants, as well as sources outside your household, and you may feel free to correct or add to our information."

The man nodded and replied, "Very good, sir."

Holmes went through Leona Pride's career and recent health issues, then asked, "Are you aware of the conditions of Miss Pride's will?"

Without missing a beat, Hawkins replied, "I am, Inspector. She updated it just two months ago. Miss Stanton and Mrs. Carlotti are to receive £300 each and I shall receive £500. All of her personal property is to be sold and the cash added to whatever is left after our bequests, then distributed to various charities after her bills and funeral expenses are met. The particulars are detailed in the document and it is on file with the firm of Fletcher & McGraw of Essex Street."

"The ladies are unaware of this," said Holmes. "Why do you know of it?"

He shrugged his shoulders, "I suppose that in a sense she considered me the man of the house and the most qualified to handle such things."

I could not help but blurt out, "The man of the house! What services did you provide to gain such trust from her?"

To his credit or his lack of shame, he did not react with anything like guilt. He merely turned to me and said, "I did whatever she asked of me, Doctor. That was what my position required."

"We have heard …" I started to accuse, but Holmes laid a hand on my arm and stopped me.

"I understand that Miss Pride received some disturbing correspondence lately. Were you aware of this?"

"Yes, Inspector. I was instructed to give the letters to the police if anything should happen to her. Now that you are here, I shall be happy to turn them over to you. If you will follow me they are in her bedroom."

We walked behind the fellow with me glaring at Holmes who merely put a finger to his lips and shook his head. He mouthed the words, "Not now!" which did little reduce my outrage, but I always do my best to obey Holmes's instructions so as not to interfere with his investigations.

Leona Pride's bedroom was fitting for one who deemed herself the 'Queen of the West End'. It was larger than the entire sitting room at Baker Street. The walls were covered in green wallpaper with a geometric pattern. The door and windows were trimmed in white. The furniture was all oak and included wardrobes on either side of the white marble fireplace. So too were the posts of the four-poster bed and a long dressing table, three drawers wide with a mirror fixed above it with various knick-knacks and a jewellery box on top. The quilted bedspread was also of the same shade of green as the wallpaper and of the same pattern. In addition it had a gold fringe along the bottom as did the bedcurtains around the upper part. There were two mauve chairs with tufted upholstery with gold trim along the bottom. Mauve-patterned rugs covered the floor. A roll-top writing desk sat by a window with gold curtains. There were several drawers but Hawkins knew exactly where to look and pulled out a large envelope filled with typewritten pages all signed by Cecil Hepworth.

As Holmes leafed through them he asked the valet, "Do you know who this *Cecil Hepworth* is?"

"Not specifically, sir. Only that he has something to do with the theatrical profession. Miss Pride claimed that he was ruining her career, but she never elaborated as to how."

Holmes handed the envelope to me and bent over to examine the typewriter. "Miss Stanton informed us that her mistress used this typewriter quite often lately, but was very insistent upon privacy when she did so. Could she have been writing to this Hepworth person?"

"It's possible I suppose, but I believe that she was writing a play of her own. She wished to remain active in the theatre as her age would soon limit her parts and, as you have been made aware, her health would soon prevent her from performing on stage."

"If she were writing a play, wouldn't the manuscript also be in this desk?" asked Holmes.

"I would presume that to be the case," answered Hawkins. "Or she may have finished it and sent it to her solicitor for safe-keeping."

Holmes said, "Let us check the drawers just in case." But as he opened the first, he suddenly began coughing and could not seem to stop. He motioned for the valet to fetch him a glass of water. When Hawkins stepped out of the room, Holmes quickly removed the cover from the typewriter, took out the ribbon spool, placed it in his pocket and re-covered the machine.

When Hawkins returned, Holmes took some healthy swallows and thanked the young man. Then he finished going through the drawers, finding no sign of a manuscript. Our next step was the dressing table where Holmes had me examine the bottles of medication laid out on top.

"These are the same as what she had on her makeup table at the theatre," said I, recalling my conversation with Fox.

"We should pack those up and have them tested, just to be sure that they are not contaminated. The snuff container also," he ordered.

Hawkins retrieved an empty box from the wardrobe and we placed the bottles and boxes within. As we prepared to leave, Holmes turned to the valet and asked, "I understand that you were also her driver. Did you take her everywhere, or were there occasions when she preferred a cab?"

Hawkins bit his lip as he lowered his head, as if trying to decide how much he should reveal about his mistress. Finally, he looked up and softly said, "There were times I would drive her to an event and then when it was over she would dismiss me as she was accepting a ride from some gentleman or other. I recall that there was also one time when she advised me that she was going out and would be gone for several hours. She never said where, or why she did not wish me to drive her. I ... assumed it was to call upon one of her gentlemen friends in confidence."

Holmes requested the name of the cab company she had used and then asked one last question, "Just out of curiosity, what are you planning to do with your £500 now that your position has ended?"

Hawkins stopped with his hand on the doorknob and there seemed to be a shadow of sorrow pass over his face. He tilted his head and said, "I've been so busy trying to put the house in order that I haven't really thought about it, Inspector. I think I would rather wait until I have it in hand and see if it speaks to me."

Chapter Six

On our return journey we stopped at a post office where Holmes dispatched a telegram. Upon arriving home, I presumed that my friend would begin experimenting on the various medicines or the snuff that we had found at Pride's house. Instead, he immediately sat and began going through the letters in the envelope that Hawkins had given us. "These are all from Cecil Hepworth," he said as he flipped through them. Then reading the top one he frowned. "He seems particularly vehement toward Miss Pride and highly critical of her acting. He says his choice of Gertrude Elliot for the role of Ophelia in his movie version of *Hamlet* was inspired by her contrast to 'your pitiful performance skills, you poor old prune'."

He then pulled a rolled-up document from his inner pocket and handed it to me, As I pressed it flat to the table I could see that it was the script for the play she had been performing in. Attached was a newspaper clipping with her notation. The very first line of the script was underlined twice with marks so violent that they nearly tore the paper.

Now is the winter of our discontent

They were not spoken by Leona Pride's role as Lady Anne, but by Richard when he was still Duke of Gloucester. I could fathom no reason for her to emphasise this particular line.

In the meantime, Holmes placed a pad of paper and a pencil on the table, pulled the table lamp close to himself and began unspooling the typewriter ribbon.[1] Holmes began slowly transcribing various sections of the ribbon. Sometimes he would skip several inches hurriedly and at other times he would devote a deep study to a particular passage. As I did not wish to interrupt his concentration, I contented myself to ponder the meaning of this dialogue being so violently marked.

Soon I chose to leave him to his task and went into the parlour to show the script to my wife while I lit up a pipe to smoke in contemplation. It was a habit that I had picked up from Holmes. He was famous for his 'three-pipe problem' sessions when calculating various possibilities in his mind. I was not nearly so successful of course, but occasionally the soothing scent of vanilla or cherry smoke would relax my mind into a state of openness where my mind's eye could wander for connections of the known facts.

My wife poured over the script, looking through all of Lady Anne's lines, but found nothing else so marked. Coming back to that first page she stared at it, then tried saying it aloud, emphasising a different word each time. Taking into consideration the angry note on the newspaper clipping, she used that tone in her readings. It was when she said, "Now is the *winter* of our discontent," that Holmes walked into the room.

"Winter indeed," he commented. "Miss Pride was not only in the winter of her career but in the winter of her life. I believe now that she desperately wanted to leave one last great performance as her final legacy."

---

[1] Although easier with modern carbon ribbons, it is possible to read what was typed on old cloth typewriter ribbons, although it may be difficult depending on the ribbon's condition and the ink used; you can often see the typed characters by holding the ribbon up to a light source and examining it closely, especially with the help of side or transmitted light. (Northwestern University School of Law, *Journal of Criminal Law and Criminology*, Vol. 63, (1972)).

"She had the female lead in what was bound to be her final play," I stated. "What more could she want?"

Before he could reply, my wife picked up the newspaper clipping and read the hand-scrawled note, "*This should be me!* Perhaps she wanted to make her mark in motion pictures as her crowning achievement."

She looked up at Holmes and added, "But how does this relate to her death, Sherlock?"

"There is a box of snuff among the items that we picked up from her home. Curiously the return address is Hurst Grove, Walton-on-Thames. That is the address of Hepworth Studios, the producers of that *Hamlet* film according to that article."

"Are you saying Hepworth sent her poisoned snuff?" I asked.

"I doubt it very much, but I would like to get all the facts to satisfy Her Majesty. I suggest that 'Reverend Shubert' and the two of you compel Inspector Hopkins to come with us tomorrow to pay Cecil Hepworth a visit and obtain the facts as he knows them."

Chapter Seven

The next morning, we arrived at Scotland Yard and found Inspector Stanley Hopkins. He was very glad to have Holmes's theory and was eager to follow up with Hepworth to get the facts. It took a while to make the 20-mile trip to Hepworth Studios in Hurst Grove, Walton-on-Thames, but we arrived by mid-morning and found Hepworth on set directing a new picture. We learned that this was common as the company often turned out as many as three films per week. Hepworth was a lean, clean-shaven man in his late thirties with an excitable persona as he bellowed out directions to his actors and stagehands.

Upon Hopkins introducing himself, 'Reverend Shubert', myself as a potential biographer of Leona Pride, and my wife, and stating our purpose, Hepworth ordered his cast and crew to break for an early lunch and invited us to a meeting room, his office being too small to accommodate our group.

Once settled around a long table, Hopkins presented the items that Holmes had provided. "Do you recognise this box, Mr. Hepworth?" He slid it across the table to the producer who picked it up curiously. "Well, that is my return address, but I have never seen this box and I certainly did not send it to Miss Pride at that address. I was not aware that she indulged in the snuff habit. It seems quite unseemly for a woman of her reputation."

"So, you deny sending it to her?" confirmed Hopkins.

"Of course I deny it! I had no reason to send her anything, and even if I had I would not typewrite the labels. I handwrite all my correspondence."

The Inspector then handed over one of the letters from the pile supposedly from Hepworth to Pride. Hepworth looked at the envelope and again denied having anything to do with it. Hopkins asked him to read the enclosed letter and he did so, then cried, "This is ridiculous! I was making a silent film and did not need the talents of a stage actress known for her powerful dialogues ... especially one so famous as would have cost me ten times as much to hire. I answered her one inquiry with a single handwritten note in which I told her that I was flattered by her interest, but that the role was not worthy of an actress of her calibre and advised her that the part was already filled. These letters have typewritten signatures. I would never send such a thing. Besides, I don't type, I have a secretary to do that and it is only for scripts and contracts."

Holmes leaned over and whispered something in Hopkins's ear who in turn, asked the gentleman, "Do you have any enemies who might wish to frame you for her murder?"

"Murder!" he exclaimed. "The papers said that she had a heart attack."

"There was poison in her snuff, which is why we had to determine if you actually sent it."

Hepworth shook his head vehemently, "I assure you, Inspector, that I had nothing to do with it!"

Hopkins looked to the rest of us. To keep up appearances as a would-be biographer, I asked a question, "Were money not an object, would you have considered her for the role of Ophelia?"

The producer shook his head, "She was too old for Ophelia. However, with the publicity her name would bring and at the right salary, she would have made a grand Lady Macbeth. I have been experimenting with an invention I call a Vivaphone[1],

---

[1] The Hepworth Vivaphone was a sound-on-disc system, developed and marketed by Hepworth Film Manufacturing Company, which was not a true synchronised sound system. The performers in their films would typically

which adds sound to motion pictures. It synchronises with the movement of the actor's lips. It would have been a great achievement for her career."

I thanked the gentleman. Hopkins said our farewells, and we returned to my home where we could speak with the Inspector in private without drawing curiosity from other officials in the Yard offices. A telegram awaited Holmes and an envelope for me had arrived from Dr. Fox. It contained a report confirming that Leona Pride's snuff box had a heavy concentration of cocaine.

Gathered around our dining table, my wife served tea while Holmes lit his pipe as he laid Pride's underlined script and the newspaper clipping with her notation on the table, along with the telegram that he had just received. He then began his denouement. "Now that we know the method of her death rules out natural causes, I believe that the evidence is conclusive as to who is the killer. This telegram is from a cab company and they verify that their driver took Leona Pride out to Walton-on-Thames on the same day the package to her was postmarked."

Hopkins spoke up at that, "Are you saying that she visited Hepworth and that he responded by sending her the poisoned snuff? So what he told us today was made up to give himself an alibi?"

Holmes frowned in disappointment at the Inspector, "Not at all! I believe every word he said because it rings true to his business perspective and her personality. He praised her talent to us. Factually, he was correct in that she was too old to play Ophelia, and that a woman of her stage presence would be wasted in a silent film considering the salary he would have to pay her. He could not have known of her throat condition and I am sure that she was too proud to tell him about it.

"She, on the other hand, saw silent films as her last hope of theatrical glory. Knowing that her voice would soon be too

---

lip sync their singing and speech to prerecorded gramophone records. Albert Blinkhorn began distributing Vivaphone films in the United States in 1913.

weak to continue on stage, she could still give her physical presence and emotional gestures to grand parts before she succumbed at last to her disease. When he politely turned her down, she being the diva that she was, took affront and decided to avenge herself upon him with her final act.

"While I could not clearly decipher all the writing from her typewriter ribbons, I was able to glean enough to prove that she had typed those letters which supposedly came from him. That was why the signature was typed and not handwritten. Sending the package to herself using the return address of Walton-on-Thames would also implicate him as the poisoner."

I saw where this was leading and lent my medical expertise to the conversation, "So, in her mentally fragile state and likely under the influence of cocaine or other painkillers, she chose to commit suicide but frame Hepworth as a murderer."

Holmes nodded, "As she indicated, and as your wife so capably intoned, 'Now was the *winter* of her discontent'. Her life was coming to an end and, because of Hepworth's refusal, she was discontented at the way it was coming about. She finished her final performance and ended her life on her own terms."

Hopkins had been taking notes and now set his pencil down and remarked, "Thank you, Mr. Holmes. I'll amend my report from natural causes to suicide and that will be the end of it. Though I imagine that the press will make up their own theories over the next few days."

Holmes held up a finger as if attempting to silence the Inspector, "I implore you to do no such thing for now, Hopkins. The Queen has engaged me in this matter and my conclusions must be reported to her first of all. I suggest that you wait until she decides what should be made public about her friend."

Then he turned to my wife, "My dear, this is where I need your services ..."

Epilogue

Sherlock Holmes, being on assignment for the Foreign Office, could not very well walk into Buckingham Palace to make his report to Her Majesty without causing a stir. Therefore, through his brother Mycroft, he arranged an audience with Queen Mary for my wife and I.

Feeling that a woman-to-woman conversation would be the most conducive to this unfortunate news, my wife gave the Queen the facts of the case as relating to Leona's Pride's mental state, illness, and actions. It was agreed by us and Holmes that the actress's sexual affairs were to be kept private so as not to tarnish her reputation before her admirer, the Queen. I was there only as an escort and to provide any medical explanation if requested.

Her Majesty was naturally saddened that her friend had sunk to such depths of despair and suffering from a fatal disease that she committed suicide. She thanked us and requested that we pass her appreciation along to Holmes as well. She also took a piece of stationery with the royal emblem and dashed off a note to Inspector Hopkins, asking us to hand deliver it to him with all due haste.

We therefore went straight from Buckingham Palace to Scotland Yard and found Hopkins at his desk working on his next case. I handed him the note which he tore open and read quickly. His eyebrows rose as he did so.

"Well, that settles that," he said with a sigh. Then he read aloud the portion the Queen had requested him to report, "Leona Pride, in the finest tradition of the theatre that 'the show must go on', summoned up the strength to give her final performance in the face of a fatal disease and succumbed to a heart attack after the show. She is to be remembered as the *Diva Regina* of the West End and one of the finest actresses of our time."

Virgo: Maiden –
Goddess of Wheat
(23rd August – 22nd September)

The Absconded Virgin

Perfectionist but self-critical. Meticulous, organised and diligent. If the world were to end tomorrow, you would want a Virgo to lead the march into the new dawn. However, the self-doubt in their head means that they are often harsher on themselves than anybody else can be.

[*The Visitation of the Virgin to St. Elizabeth* (top)
and *The Flight into Egypt* (bottom)
both by Goossen van der Weyden]

204

Chapter One

It was early May 1882, according to my diary, when a visitor arrived at our door just as Holmes and I were stepping out for lunch, our landlady being away for a few days. The fellow burst out of a cab several feet away from us and came rushing along the pavement towards us at a pace which he was not built to maintain. He was an elderly gentleman of perhaps sixty years, short, fat and red in the face from even this brief exertion. He stopped before us and gasped, "Are one of you gentlemen Mr. Sherlock Holmes, the detective?"

"I am he," answered Holmes. "But I suggest that you first avail yourself of the services of my colleague here, Dr. John Watson."

The fellow bent over, placing his hands on his thighs to catch his breath. As he did so, I stepped forward and hooked my hand around his left arm to help him into the house. Once we had him seated in Mrs. Hudson's entrance hall, I went to the kitchen to fetch him a glass of water. When I returned, the gentleman had removed his hat, unbuttoned his coat and loosened his collar. Holmes was standing before him in quiet contemplation.

Our visitor took the water from me with a grateful nod. When he appeared ready to talk, Holmes began the conversation. "What can we do for you, Mr. Franklin Payne? Is there something amiss at the National Gallery, or does this involve a more personal calamity?"

Payne sat up straight at this revelation. I had seen Holmes perform this act on multiple occasions, so it was no surprise to me but, due to our visitor's weakened state I nudged my friend and said, "You'd better explain it to him. He's in no fit state for further surprises."

Holmes gestured towards the man's bowler and declared, "Your name is neatly inscribed inside your hat and the chain of your pocket watch bears a fob with the emblem of The National Gallery. As this is only given to employees, I deduce that you work there and by your age and bearing I would venture to say that you are either a member of the board of directors or one of the curators. So, again I ask, how may we help you?"

Payne heaved a sigh and replied, "Yes, I am the curator of Renaissance art for the Gallery. I am pleased to see that your observational skills were not exaggerated to me. We wish you to put them to use to discover how one of our paintings was stolen and attempt to retrieve it."

"And who described my skills to you, if I may ask?"

"A mutual friend, Professor Wooley[1] at the British Museum. This has the same delicacy as the case you solved for him. If I go to the police, the theft becomes public record and could affect our ability to obtain artworks on loan from various donors."

Holmes nodded his understanding and asked, "What was stolen and when?"

"Three years ago, Mrs. Joseph Green donated two panels from the life of the Virgin Mary by Goossen van der Weyden, a Flemish artist of the Renaissance era. They have been rotating on display and were brought out again just three weeks ago. One of them was *The Visitation of the Virgin to St. Elizabeth*. The other was *The Flight to Egypt*. Sometime last night the latter was removed from the display and cannot be found."

"How large is it?" asked the detective.

---

[1] Professor Montgomery Wooley was a mentor of Holmes and had called upon his services in the case of the *Olive Garden Painting* in *The Colourful Cases of Sherlock Holmes, Volume One* by Roger Riccard and published by Baker Street Studios Limited in 2022.

"It's just over 31 inches by 27 inches, and it is oil on wood, so it can't just be rolled up like a piece of canvas."

"When was the last time it was seen in place?"

Payne wiped his forehead with a large kerchief and replied, "It was there last night at closing time. I walked through that section on my way out and saw it myself. But when I came in this morning, it was gone and there was a different painting in its place."

"A different painting?" I asked. "What was it?"

"This one was about the same size, but it was oil on canvas. I had to look it up. It was not an original but a good copy of a painting by Elisabetta Sirani, an Italian Renaissance painter. It's called *Virgin and Child*. The original would date back to 1663, but this looks like it was done only recently. The colours are too vibrant and the canvas appears to be of recent manufacture."

This development struck me and I asked incredulously, "You mean that someone not only stole a piece of wood over two feet square but also brought in a canvas painting of equal size without being seen?"

The curator hung his head in embarrassment, then looked up forlornly at us to reply, "I'm afraid that is exactly what has happened. Would you please come and investigate, Mr. Holmes? The Gallery will pay any fee or expenses you require to regain this treasured work of art."

I knew that the extraordinary aspects of the crime would appeal to my friend and was not surprised in the least when he replied, "I shall be happy to look into the matter for you, Mr. Payne. Watson, are you game?"

"I wouldn't miss it," I replied. I had been Holmes's flatmate for over two years at this point and had grown accustomed, indeed even joyful, at the opportunities to share his cases. I had thought my wartime experience in Afghanistan had given me my fill of adventure for a lifetime, but since my return to civilian life in the company of this brilliant, if eccentric, detective, I had found the rush of adventure to be intoxicating and craved its distraction from dull daily routines.

It was less than three miles to the National Gallery at Trafalgar Square, and the cabbie who had brought Payne returned the three of us there in good time.

Holmes had to caution Payne to enter the facility slowly so as not to call the attention he so wanted to avoid. Still, even making the effort to walk at a normal pace, the chubby little man was wringing his hands the whole time.

We entered the Renaissance Room and found just a scattering of people wandering about and appreciating the various works. There were small groups gathered around Michelangelo and Da Vinci exhibits. The rest of the visitors were wandering about alone or in pairs. As we approached, one couple was admiring the Goossen van der Weyden pair of paintings, unaware that one of them had been substituted.

"I like that one better, John," said the young woman to her gentleman escort, pointing at the Sirani. "The colours are brighter and the close-up shows their facial features better."

I did not see a wedding ring so I presumed that he was her suitor as they were of about the same age. He tilted his head and nodded, "I agree, Elizabeth. It's almost as if they were done by two different artists. Perhaps that one is from later in his career as his skills improved. He smiled and took a step closer, she following with her arm hooked around his as he continued, "Yes, that one is on canvas and the other is on wood. Definitely from two different stages of his career."

Payne was listening to this conversation and holding his breath in fear that the substitution was about to be revealed. Holmes stepped forward, however, and remarked, "You are correct, sir. That one on canvas is from decades later than the other."[2]

The man called John gave Holmes an appreciative look at his deduction being confirmed in front of his lady. Then he smiled and said, "Thank you, sir." He gave the painting one more look, smiled and then suggested to his companion that they move along to the Raphael exhibit.

---

[2] In fact, it was done at least 120 years later.

Payne stepped forward and sighed, "Thank you, Mr. Holmes. I thought we were surely about to be exposed."

"If you were so fearful of that why is the painting still hanging here?" asked the detective.

"Visitors were already coming in by the time I noticed the substitution," replied the curator. "I did not want to draw attention to it by taking it down."

Holmes frowned, "Your logic escapes me. I suggest that we remove it immediately and take it somewhere that I can conduct a thorough examination."

Chapter Two

Having the three of us there gave the appearance of the removal of the painting being an official act, so little attention was paid by the visitors in the gallery. Payne was so nervous that I carried the artwork as the curator led us to a workroom where masterpieces were in various stages of restoration or cleaning.

I set the painting down on a table and Holmes immediately turned it over to examine the back. What we saw there was a surprise to all of us. Rather than the normal wooden frame over which a canvas would be stretched, there was a solid, aged, wooden panel, such as one might expect to see in early Renaissance works.

Holmes gave a questioning gaze to the curator, "In my studies with Professor Wooley, I never came across a technique where a canvas was stretched over a solid panel. Was this ever tried when canvas first began to be used?"

Payne shook his head, "If so it would have been at the very beginning of canvas usage. I've never seen it, and it certainly would have been discontinued by the time the original of this painting was done."

Holmes nodded, "Then I suggest that we see what lies beneath."

Carefully he removed the art from its frame. Examining the edges of the artwork he said, "Notice the new staples holding the canvas to the wood. This was certainly done recently."

He pulled out his multiplex knife and began prying loose the staples, starting at the top of the canvas and after working a few inches down one side, he could pull the canvas away from the wood enough to see what was beneath.

Payne gasped, "It's *The flight into Egypt*! Thank God it's still here!"

Holmes continued to pull more staples off until the whole painting was visible. Payne peered at it closely and cried, "It is undamaged! How wonderful!" Then he stopped and asked the question on all our minds, "But why this ruse, Mr. Holmes? What purpose could there be in covering it up instead of stealing it?"

Holmes was stroking his chin in thought, then remarked, "In the case of the attempted theft from Professor Wooley, the thieves offered to buy the fake painting, knowing that there was a masterpiece underneath. But you say you've received no ransom demand or any other communication?"

"No, but it's only been a few hours."

"Then I suggest we put this back together and rehang it as quickly as possible before our culprit realises that we have discovered the truth. If he thinks the gallery is leaving it in place to cover up a theft, he may continue with his plan."

"What do you imagine that plan to be, Mr. Holmes?"

"Off the top of my head, I can theorise at least three possibilities. Given time to contemplate, I am sure other scenarios will come to mind. For now, we return it as it was and see what our perpetrator's next move shall be. Once he reveals his plan, we can strategise a counter-manoeuvre."

He quickly reassembled the artwork, and we returned it to the exhibit. While he was working, he asked Payne, "Do you have any recently dismissed employees or someone disgruntled with the Gallery?"

Payne frowned, his fat lower lip protruding like a child pouting, "We've dismissed no one for a long time, and I am not aware of any disgruntled employee or patron. Certainly, no public complaints have been made of late."

I posed a question of my own, "If this exhibit has been up for three weeks, why did the, I guess that we should refer to him as 'forger', wait until now to make the substitution? Is there anything unique about the timing?"

"Nothing I can think of, Doctor," replied Payne. "Certainly there was nothing different last night than any other night since the exhibit opened."

Holmes commented on that remark, "It suggests that the forger was not ready to make the substitution until last night. That could very well mean that it took that much time for him to create the false Sirani."

"But how did he make the substitution?" exclaimed Payne, slamming his chubby fist into a fleshy palm with a dull thud. The Gallery is locked at night, and there are guards at all the entrances."

"Do these guards make rounds of the displays during the night?" asked the detective.

"There is no need," replied the curator. "They make rounds at closing time to ensure that everyone has left the building, and once the doors are locked they maintain their posts until morning. In addition there are two guards marching around the outside perimeter to prohibit anyone attempting to gain access through a window or vandalise the building."

"Are any of the guards new?"

"No, Mr. Holmes, and they are all ex-military or former police officers above reproach."

Holmes contemplated that for a moment and then asked, "The restoration room we were just in, is that locked at night?"

"No, with the building secure and guarded, everything in there is perfectly safe."

"Is there someone in it at all times during the day?"

"Yes, there could be anywhere from two to half a dozen people working in there, depending on the inventory, and they stagger their breaks so that it is never empty."

"And you suspect none of those men?"

"They have worked with us for years and are some of the most reputable men in their field. It is unthinkable that any of them would do such a thing."

Holmes frowned, "In my line of work, Mr. Payne, it is often the 'unthinkable' that turns out to be true. I should like to return to that room and make a thorough examination this evening after the staff have left."

"We close at six o'clock. You should be able to work in there after that undisturbed."

"That shall be fine," replied my companion. "Watson and I must return to Baker Street while I explore some possibilities, but we shall return before closing time. If you hear from the forger, send for me immediately."

Chapter Three

On our way home we made a detour to consume the lunch we had been detained from, though Holmes ate sparingly and also sent off a telegram. Upon returning to Baker Street, he sat down to a quick review of the afternoon papers, then lit his pipe for what I presumed would be a session of contemplation and theorising. Before I left him to his task, however, I asked him who he had telegraphed.

"I have an acquaintance who dabbles in the world of questionable art where he picks up bargains for his own collection. He has occasional run-ins with forgers and I have asked him his thoughts on the matter at hand. He may be able to point us to someone gifted in Sirani's style."[1]

"I still don't understand why the substitution rather than an actual theft? What does the forger gain?"

"That will be my precise subject of cogitation for the next hour and a quarter, Watson. If you will excuse me?"

Knowing Holmes's methods, I suspected that we might be in for a long night, so I thought it prudent to take an afternoon nap in preparation while he contemplated his multi-pipe problem. When I awoke some two hours later, I found him gone with a note left for me.

---

[1] This was likely Charles Robie, whom Watson would later meet in 1887 during the case of *The Crisis of Count Vermillion* in *The Colourful Cases of Sherlock Holmes, Volume 4* published by Baker Street Studios Limited in 2025.

> *Watson, have returned to Gallery in disguise. Meet me there at your convenience, but no later than 5:30. - S.H.*

Our landlady, Mrs. Hudson, had left us a well-stocked pantry, and I made up a sandwich and washed it down with a small beer before setting off, assuming that Holmes, per his habit when on a case, had taken no account of any time for dinner.

Arriving at the Gallery, I began my search for my friend. Not having gained the skills necessary to penetrate his disguises, I could only assume he would be somewhere near the van der Weyden exhibit, and that he would contact me when the time was right.

I strolled about for a few minutes, then took a seat on a nearby bench and watched the other visitors. Among those were a few apparent art students, sketch pads in hand, making drawings of various masterpieces. One fellow I noted had several sketches of the hands in many of these works, showing their varied positions and musculature. To my surprise, he came and sat near me on the bench, putting the finishing touches on a particular set of lady's fingers. He was about my age, but heavier, and sported a thin moustache and goatee beard of jet black. His clothes were somewhat loose-fitting and appeared to be more for comfort than style. Upon his head, he wore a large beret, typical to those of many Dutch artists. After a few seconds, he turned his sketch pad towards me and, in a voice that was unmistakably Holmes's with a Dutch accent, said, "Pardon me, sir. My name is Joseph Vernet. May I ask what you think of these?"

He had said this with a wink of his eye, and I played along, pretending to study his sketches. "You appear to have added more detail than the original artist," I remarked. "I see blisters, callouses, bruises, cuts and scars that are not shown in the paintings here."

"Ah, yes," he replied. "I have chosen to include what would be typical of the occupations of those individuals the original artist put into his or her works. I believe details are essential to accuracy."

"Well, you have certainly captured more detail than the original artist."

'Vernet' smiled, "Thank you. My art requires such attention."

I knew that the 'art' he was talking about was the science of observation and deduction. He would often explain to me how a person's occupation could be deduced by physical characteristics, especially hands.

"Have you discovered many new details in your visit here today?" I asked.

Keeping his voice low he said, "I have been keeping track of those who seem especially interested in the compromised exhibit. I believe that someone skilful enough to produce that forgery of Sirani, is egotistical enough to wish to view it on display and to note others appreciating it. I would be very surprised if he did not return to the scene of his crime."

"Has any such person come to your attention?"

"Only one since I returned. They may have been here earlier today or while I was gone. I shall keep this up for a few days, if necessary, to see if anyone falls into a pattern. In the meantime, I wish to conduct an experiment at closing time and could use your assistance."

At six o'clock I did as he had instructed me and then left the building for a pre-arranged meeting with Mr. Payne at a nearby restaurant where we ate a light dinner. Payne questioned me considerably during the meal, but I could only assure him that my friend was working diligently on his case and was making progress. At seven-fifteen, we finished our food, and I informed him that we needed to return to the Gallery at Holmes's request to see the results of an experiment that he had conducted.

Upon our entrance, Payne instructed the guard at the front door to admit Holmes upon his arrival. I then led him to the exhibit where the forgery was hanging. To his great surprise, the Sirani was no longer on the wall. In its place was a Caravaggio Biblical scene. However, this one seemed to be in stages of cleaning as portions of it were darker than others.

Payne put his hands to the sides of his head and cried out, "What is this?"

Immediately Holmes stepped out from behind a column to pacify the much-tried curator. "Fear not, Mr. Payne. I merely borrowed one of the works in your Restoration Room for this little experiment. We will return the Sirani and continue our ruse. But I wanted to see how easy it would be for someone to stay behind after closing time to make the switch. I had Watson speak to the last of your restorers as he left, while I snuck in the door behind them. I hid in a back cupboard for a short time, to ensure that no guard would see me while they were checking and making sure that the place was empty. Once I gave them enough time to return to their posts, I merely picked up one of the works being cleaned and substituted it for the Sirani until Watson brought you back here for my demonstration."

"So how does this solve our case, Mr. Holmes?" asked the curator with some asperity in his voice.

Holmes folded his arms across his chest and looked down upon the shorter man, "It proves how the deed was done. As it turns out, my hiding place in the restoration cupboard was the same as that of our thief. I found a crumpled paper wrapper and crumbs from a sandwich that he ate while hiding in there all night until he could slip out the next morning when the Gallery re-opened."

"But surely my staff would have seen him exit the cupboard."

The detective shook his head, "He would have left his hiding place just before the morning opening and likely hid in one of the public water closets until he could leave and blend in with the morning visitors. Remember, the man is an artist. That implies great patience and intelligence."

"What now?" asked Payne.

"Now we put the painting back, and I continue my surveillance of the visitors. I have other avenues which I am exploring, and Watson will be relaying any messages from those sources which may help us identify our man."

"I cannot keep that Sirani in place forever. Someone is bound to notice and raise an inquiry."

"I believe we should not need to do so for more than one or two more days. Then you may return the *Flight into Egypt* to its rightful place.

Chapter Four

Upon our return to Baker Street, Holmes found a handwritten note slipped under the door in response to his telegram. While curious, I was not so ill-mannered as to attempt to read over his shoulder. The quick glimpse I had of the document only showed me a paragraph at the top and bottom and what appeared to be names and notes in a list in the middle.

The notes apparently included addresses and Holmes advised me that he would be going out for the evening to investigate. I asked if I should come with him, but he declined my offer, instead asking that I plan on spending the day near him at the Gallery on the morrow. As my practice of medicine was not a busy one in those days, I readily agreed, and we left it at that until morning.

While Holmes rarely eats a full meal during an investigation, he has learned that my constitution is not so inclined as to skip meals, and he awoke me in time to eat a healthy breakfast before we set out for the Gallery. As I partook of some sausages, eggs and toast, washed down by tea, I questioned him about his evening excursions.

"I was able to get a look at several of the men on the list, so if they show up at the Gallery, I can observe their behaviour regarding the forgery. There were three men whom I did not find at home or were unable to observe. I shall try them again after the Gallery closes today."

Once at the Gallery, Holmes, in his disguise as a Dutch art student, kept up his sketching in the Renaissance Room while I wandered about the neighbouring exhibits, always within sight of my friend should the need arise. It was just before eleven o'clock when he gave me a discreet signal, and I met him at the bench we had occupied the previous day.

"Watson, please inform Mr. Payne to have a guard standing by and be ready to assist me should I meet any resistance."

"You've identified your man?" I asked, gazing about the room, but seeing no one who stood out.

"I believe so, but I wish to have you and a guard at the ready should he make a break for it when I confront him."

I returned within two minutes with Payne and a uniformed guard. When Holmes observed us, he walked up to a young man who now seemed familiar to me. Then I recalled, it was the fellow who had been there with his lady the previous morning.

Holmes walked slowly up to him as he admired the Sirani and asked in his Dutch accent, as he extended his hand. "Excuse me, I am Joseph Vernet. Are you John Blake?"

Blake, surprised at this stranger knowing his name, hesitantly shook hands, "I am, sir. But how did you know?"

At Holmes's nod of verification, Payne, the guard and I closed in and surrounded the fellow. "We have been admiring your work these last two days and wish to discuss it with you." Blake tried to pull away but Holmes's grip was like a vice and I grabbed the fellow's other arm and whispered into his ear, "Let's not have a fuss. Just come along quietly before you cause any more trouble."

Seeing his situation as untenable, Blake cooperated as we marched him to Payne's office. The guard remained outside the door while Payne, Holmes and I stood over the young man whom I had set down into a chair.

Holmes removed his beret and facial hair and said, "My name is Sherlock Holmes, and this is my colleague, Dr. John Watson. Mr. Payne is the curator of this exhibit and he hired us to find out who substituted the forged Sirani for the *Flight into Egypt.*"

"What does that have to do with me?" asked Blake calmly.

Holmes gave one of his quick little smiles and then sat on the corner of Payne's desk. "Because you, sir, came in here the day before yesterday with the forged Sirani canvas rolled up, likely in your trouser leg. You creeped into the restoration room at closing time and hid there until the guards had ensured that all visitors had left for the day. You then went out and absconded the painting off the wall, took it back to the restoration room, where you removed its frame and placed your own canvas over the original. You reframed the painting, accidentally cutting your finger on one of the staples as you did so."

Blake could not but help gaze down at his left forefinger where a small cut had scabbed over.

"You then re-hung the painting. You could not exit the building until it re-opened to the public the next morning, so you took up residence in the restoration room cupboard where you ate a sandwich. You left your wrapping behind and likely did not notice that you had gotten some of your blood on the paper. You left after the building opened and then returned that afternoon with your friend Elizabeth. You may recall it was I who told you that the new painting was several decades newer than the other van der Weyden. I noted your smile at the time but did not attach any importance to it. I merely thought that you were satisfied that you were correct. It did not occur to me that you were actually gloating over your trick.

"We discovered that the substitution merely covered the original and that it had not been stolen. However, we left it intact in the hope that the forger might return to admire his work. You did so and here we are."

After such a thorough explanation, Blake could hardly deny his involvement. But after a moment, he asked, "But how did you know who I was and that I had done it?"

My friend replied, "I have sources on the shadier side of the art world. Your name was on a list given to me, and when I saw you here for the second day in a row, having heard you being called 'John' by your lady friend, and with the cut on your hand, the deduction seemed logical. You had come to admire your work. My only question for you now is why? Obviously, theft was not a motive."

With false bravado, Blake retorted, "First, let me ask, what is my crime? As nothing has been stolen, by what right do you hold me? You could easily have restored the original yourselves."

Payne puffed out his already puffy cheeks and cried, "You have committed fraud on the public and desecrated a masterpiece! You could have ruined a priceless work of art!"

Blake raised a hand and pointed his finger upwards, "Ah, but I did not ruin it and I did not desecrate it, I merely covered it over temporarily. In fact, it was you who committed fraud by leaving it up after you discovered the truth. What would the newspapers think of that, I wonder? 'Curator Fails to Recognise Masterpiece Substitution'. Wouldn't that make a sensational headline?"

Payne's face turned so red I thought that he might have an apoplexy, and so I guided him into his chair and poured him some water from the carafe on his desk. Turning to our culprit I said, "You really need to explain yourself, my good man. What will Miss Elizabeth think of you should this incident become public?"

Blake bowed his head, nodding slowly. Finally, he looked up and said, "It was for her sake that I did it."

Holmes folded his arms over his chest and declared, "Please continue, Mr. Blake."

He took a deep breath and told his tale. "Elizabeth is to be my fiancée. She is a devout Catholic, as am I. However, her sensibilities are even more strict than my own. She has been asking me for some time to bring her to the National Gallery. While I knew that would expose her to a variety of both male and female nudes, I felt that she could handle that in the name of art. What would be too much for her, in my mind, was the exposure of the Virgin Mary's bare breast in the act of feeding the Christ child on *The Flight into Egypt*. She holds Mary in extremely high regard, in fact, it is her middle name. To expose any nakedness of the Blessed Virgin would be extremely offensive to her. Thus, I covered it up on the day I knew we would be coming.

"I was very surprised that it was still on display today, and I was prepared to write an anonymous letter to the gallery explaining where the original was so the exhibit could be restored."

After much arguing back and forth, it was finally agreed that no charges would be filed against Blake and no reports to the press would appear against Payne. The van der Weyden painting was restored to its proper condition immediately after this meeting and the forged Sirani was returned to Blake with a warning from Holmes that he should use his talents to produce his own works and avoid the world of art forgery if he expected to have a happy life with his bride to be.

Blake did go on to start up his own studio where he sold copies of masterpieces, clearly labelled as such, as well as many fine works of his own.

Coming Soon

The Zodiac Cases of Sherlock Holmes

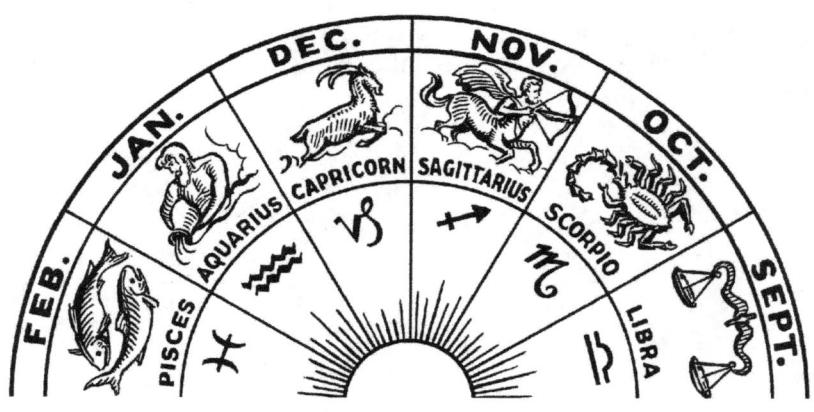

Volume 2

By

Roger Riccard

www.ingramcontent.com/pod-product-compliance
Lightning Source LLC
Chambersburg PA
CBHW061133200626
46817CB00016B/1319